MR. DARCY, THE BEAST

A PRIDE AND PREJUDICE VARIATION

THE HAPPILY EVER COLLECTION, BOOK ONE

Valerie Lennox

Punk Rawk Books

MR. DARCY, THE BEAST
© 2019 by Valerie Lennox
www.vjchambers.com

Punk Rawk Books

ISBN: 9781677761050
Printed in the United States of America

10 9 8 7 6 5 4 3 2 1

MR. DARCY, THE BEAST

A PRIDE AND PREJUDICE VARIATION

THE HAPPILY EVER COLLECTION, BOOK ONE

Valerie Lennox

CHAPTER ONE

"Gentleman *are* scarce," exclaimed Miss Elizabeth Bennet to those gathered around her. Her sisters, Jane and Catherine, who they called Kitty, and her friend Miss Charlotte Lucas, were all standing close by in their evening dresses. Kitty was drinking some of the punch, rather too much of it, Elizabeth thought, because it was a bit heavy on the wine, and Kitty was giggling overmuch.

Even now, Kitty was giggling. She had not stopped, in fact, Elizabeth thought, for the last ten minutes.

Elizabeth was in attendance at a public ball in Meryton along with her family. She had come with the intent of dancing as much as possible, but the problem was that eligible women outnumbered all the willing men for dancing, and so she had spent at least two dances on the sidelines.

"Lizzy," admonished Jane, "you cannot simply go and speak to him. You have not been introduced."

"You are only pouring cold water over the enterprise because you had two dances with the new master of Netherfield," said Elizabeth. "And besides, your dance card is always full, because you are the pretty one." She laughed to let her sister know that she was only jesting, that there was no malice in her words, and indeed, there were not. Elizabeth would not want to be the pretty one. She would rather be the one with the witty tongue.

Kitty was still giggling.

"Be that as it may," said Charlotte, "your sister is correct.

You cannot speak to a man you have not been introduced to."

"I have thought of that," said Elizabeth, "and I think that Jane must go and speak to Mr. Bingley, her new admirer, and beg that we all get an introduction."

"Oh, Lizzy, no, might you leave me out of it?" said Jane. "There must be some reason that gentleman is hiding in the corner."

As she spoke, they all turned to look into the shadows where the gentleman in question was standing, and they grew quiet. Even Kitty did, the laughter dying in her throat.

The gentleman had trailed behind the rest of his party when he'd arrived. Mr. Bingley, his two sisters, and his sister's husband, had all stepped into the light, but the other gentleman, he'd kept his head down, behind his hat, which he had not taken off upon arrival, which was highly irregular, even improper.

He didn't seem to be wearing his hat now, Elizabeth noted, but it was impossible to tell from here. He stood in the corner, away from the lights, and there was no way to make out his face.

"I have heard his name is Mr. Darcy," said Charlotte.

"Who did you have that from?" whispered Kitty, breathless.

"I can't be sure," said Charlotte. "Perhaps Mrs. Harrington."

"I heard that he has ten thousand a year," said Elizabeth.

"Must we gossip so about him?" said Jane. "He obviously wants his privacy."

"Gentleman are scarce, darling Jane," said Elizabeth. "What excuse does he have for not dancing with *anyone*? If you will not ask Mr. Bingley for an introduction, I shall do it myself. Mr. Bingley seems quite genial, and I do not think he will deny me."

"Oh, indeed, he would not. No one would," said Jane. "But it is so very forward."

"Lizzy is always thus," said Kitty, giggling again.

"That is not the case," said Elizabeth. "I am not always forward." But then the music stopped and the current dance was over. "Oh, now is my chance, there is no music. I must find Mr. Bingley before he begins another dance." She pushed herself up on tiptoes, looking until she saw the man. "Excuse me, all of you. There he is."

"Lizzy!" said Jane. "Please."

But Elizabeth did not listen. She was already darting through the crowd to find Mr. Bingley. When she reached him, she realized that the other girls had all followed, even Jane.

"Miss Bennet!" said Mr. Bingley, addressing Jane and not Elizabeth. His cheeks were rosy and he was a little bit out of breath, still recovering from the last dance. He was smiling widely, though, in fine spirits.

"Mr. Bingley," responded Jane, bowing her head and looking shy.

"Mr. Bingley," said Elizabeth, "I wonder if I could beg a favor of you, sir."

Mr. Bingley turned to her. "Miss Elizabeth, if it is within my ability to grant, I would be most pleased to do so."

Elizabeth gestured. "The gentleman in the corner? Might we have an introduction?"

"Oh," said Bingley, smiling even more widely. "Is that all? Well, certainly, of course. I am so terribly sorry that he is staying out of the way. I thought I had talked him into coming out into society a bit, but he is being most disagreeable. Truly, though, it is perhaps his first ball since the accident, and I suppose I see why he is feeling hesitant." He looked over at Mr. Darcy in the shadows and then back to Elizabeth. "You know, Miss Elizabeth, I do wonder if it might be a bit much for him, all four of you at once?"

"Is he quite shy, sir?" said Elizabeth, who was now bursting at the seams with curiosity about this man.

"He has been in mourning for some time," said Mr.

Bingley. "He lost his younger sister tragically. He doted on her."

"Oh," said Elizabeth, feeling some of her mirth drain away. "Why, how awful. I am deeply sorry."

"Perhaps if I only brought one of you to introduce," said Mr. Bingley. "Perhaps that would not overwhelm him?"

"All right," said Elizabeth, looking back at the other girls.

Kitty took this opportunity to giggle again.

Everyone glared at her, and she stopped.

Jane spoke up, her voice soft. "If the gentlemen is in such poor spirits, perhaps we ought to leave him alone."

"No, he is in want of cheering," said Bingley. "I brought him here in the hopes that he might…" He sighed. "Well, perhaps you can lift his spirits, Miss Elizabeth. Would you?"

Elizabeth's lips parted. She had meant to scold the man, but now she was unsure of her approach. "I can try."

"That is all anyone can ask of himself," said Bingley. "Come with me, then."

"Lizzy," said Jane quietly. "Don't be harsh with him."

"I won't," said Elizabeth, feeling a bit nervous now. Was she always harsh, then? If so, she was not sure that she could help it.

Mr. Bingley had already started across the room. He looked back at her.

She lifted her skirts to take quick steps to catch up.

They walked together.

"Listen," said Mr. Bingley, "there is… well, he is self-conscious about his countenance."

"Oh, indeed?" Elizabeth did not know how to respond to this. Was Mr. Darcy frightfully ugly or something?

"If you would … don't stare," said Mr. Bingley. "Although I know you would not. I can see, even in our brief acquaintance, that you are a well-bred and polite young lady, just as your elder sister is, and she is…" Mr. Bingley sighed a little. "Oh, your *sister*, Miss Elizabeth."

"Yes," said Elizabeth. "She is quite the loveliest sister a

girl could ask for." There was no way not to love Jane. She was goodness personified.

Mr. Bingley chuckled. "I am sorry. I must school my tongue, I believe. You will think me quite rude to express myself thus."

"Of course not, sir," said Elizabeth.

And then they were close, and Mr. Darcy loomed.

She could only make out the edges of his jacket, the ends of his cravat. His neck and shoulders and face were entirely in shadow.

They slowed and then came to a stop. They were closer, but she still could not make out his features. She only knew that he was tall, quite tall, and that his shoulders were broad, but his waist was tapered. He was formidable but appealing.

Elizabeth felt even more nervous now.

"Darcy," said Mr. Bingley. "I wonder if I might present to you Miss Elizabeth Bennet?"

"You can't be serious, Bingley," came the rumble of a voice from the corner. "I would be outside in the carriage if it were not so dreadfully cold. Indeed, I would be back at Netherfield if you had not pestered me to accompany you, and I would be holed up in Pemberley if you had not drowned me in letters begging for a visit. It seems to me that you are always asking for more. Cannot you be satisfied with any of my offerings?"

Bingley cleared his throat. "I must apologize for Mr. Darcy, I'm afraid."

"No, indeed, it is not at all a problem," said Elizabeth, squinting a bit, trying to see any hint of Mr. Darcy's countenance, but unable to see anything. "I understand fully. Mr. Darcy has a great many grievances against you, Mr. Bingley. You have been rather a wonderful friend to him, and I can see why he must resent that greatly."

Mr. Bingley laughed a bit, but looked uncomfortable. "Now, now, Miss Elizabeth, you do not understand Mr. Darcy's position—"

" No, you are right. " Elizabeth regretted the words immediately. Her previous statement had been too sarcastic. She was meant to be kind to this strange man. "I should not have said such a thing. I was too hard on your friend. I do not know him. Indeed, I cannot know him, for I cannot even be introduced, and surely that must mean that his situation is quite dire. I cannot understand any of it, and I should not have spoken in such a manner. I do apologize, sir. I am quite sorry for what I said. I should have thought before I said it."

"No, no," said Mr. Bingley. "Mr. Darcy, please. Will you be introduced to the young lady? Why have you come to a ball if you will not see anyone or speak to anyone?"

"Yes, I must admit," said Elizabeth, "it is a strange way to occupy oneself in company."

A chuckle from the darkness. "Yes, I suppose it is I who should apologize. Of course I will be introduced. It is a great pleasure to meet you, Miss Bennet. And I would not censure what you have said. You are correct, of course. You have spoken it all rather well and rather quickly. Indeed, I wish my horse had the speed of thy tongue."

Elizabeth pursed her lips. She did not know him well enough to be certain whether he meant the words ironically or not, but she did recognize the quote. "Why, Sir Benedick means that as an insult in the play, Mr. Darcy."

"Does he?" said Mr. Darcy. "Well, I assure you, I meant it sincerely. I should be quite happy to listen to you talk, Miss Bennet. Not only because I enjoy the subject of your speech, but your voice has rather a pleasing tone. You have come here to meet me, so will you consent to stay and talk a while? Was that your desire when you came to me?"

"Well, if I am honest," said Elizabeth, "I came to ask why a man would refuse to dance at a ball when there are not nearly enough gentleman to go round." She cringed. "But I have been instructed not to be so with you, and to be lively, and been told that you have reasons for your melancholy, and so I should have not said that either. I am not sure, sir, if it is the speed of my tongue that is to be blamed or the sluggishness of my wit."

Mr. Darcy laughed again.

Mr. Bingley was looking back and forth between them, seemingly a bit confuddled. He turned to Darcy. " I say, Darcy, I would have you dance. That is why we are here. I brought you here for that purpose exclusively."

"And would Miss Bennet wish to dance with me?" said Mr. Darcy.

"Is that a request, sir?" said Elizabeth.

" Perhaps you would care to see what you would be agreeing to dance with before giving an answer," said Mr. Darcy, and he stepped forward, and the lamplight spread across his face, and Elizabeth barely managed to stifle a sound of surprise.

Mr. Darcy ' s face was badly scarred. His nose was crooked as though it had been broken in several places, and his skin was a mass of twisting, pink, and painful flesh. One eye and one cheek were unmarred, and she could see that he had once been a handsome man with a strong visage. There was still a haughty look in his eyes.

Elizabeth knew she had been told not to stare, but it seemed equally as rude to look away, so she lifted her chin and met his gaze steadily. "I would be quite happy to dance with you, sir."

"Ah, but you would say, as Benedick does, 'By this light, I take thee for pity,'" said Mr. Darcy. "So, I think I shall not dance." He retreated into the shadows again. "In fact, I think I shall go back to the carriage after all, never mind the cold."

* * *

"Darcy," came Bingley's voice, and then his hand on his friend's shoulder.

Mr. Darcy stopped walking, but he did not turn to face Mr. Bingley. He was outside the ball, back in his coat and hat, and he was only steps from the coach. The air out here was cold, but it was not so punishing as he might expect. He could bear it.

"I am sorry," said Bingley. "I should not have done that."

"No, I should not have come," said Darcy.

"I should not have pushed you," said Bingley. "I only thought it would do you good, a bit of fun. You have had no pleasure in nine months, I daresay."

Darcy did turn to look at him. "It is not your fault. I thought perhaps I could..." He trailed off. It had seemed possible when he and Bingley had been discussing it in the drawing room at Netherfield. After all, it was not as though this was some high society ball in London amongst the ton. This was only a small country gathering with country gentlemen and their daughters. Bingley was right. If there was a place and a time to ease his way back amongst others, this was the place to do it.

But then they arrived, and he knew it was impossible.

"It is your pride," said Bingley. "But I tell you, it does not matter. One dance—"

"They would be whispering about me all night," said Mr. Darcy. "I'm sorry, no, I can't bear it."

"You are being ridiculous," said Bingley. "No one would care. You are Darcy of Pemberley, and these women are good and kind souls, who would be more interested in who you are than your face. I tell you, it does not matter."

Darcy didn't say anything.

"I hesitate to say anything, but you are hiding out of vanity—"

"Please, Bingley," said Darcy. "You do not know of what you speak. Besides, I feel I must find somewhere to sit down." His injuries had not only scarred his face, but damaged his leg as well. He had gone without his cane for the night, but he regretted it now, especially outside. The cold was making him ache.

"We shall leave," said Bingley. "We'll be off at once."

"No, don't trouble yourself," said Darcy. "I'll go back to

Netherfield and send the carriage back for you and the others. The distance is not so far as to prohibit that."

"If that is what you wish," said Mr. Bingley.

"It is," said Mr. Darcy. In the end, it wasn't the injuries themselves that pained him so much. Nor was it the scars. It wasn't the physical pain either. It was only that it was all there, written across his face as a permanent reminder of his failure. It was a sign of the fact that he was less than a man, that he was unable to complete his duties, and that he was worthless.

* * *

Elizabeth was waiting at the doorway to the assembly when Mr. Bingley returned alone. "I am so very sorry," she said to him. "I chased him away, did I not?"

"It is not your fault," said Mr. Bingley. "I did not properly prepare you. I should have told you what to expect. And perhaps I should not have insisted upon his attendance tonight as well."

"You did prepare me," said Elizabeth. "You told me that he had been in mourning, that he was embarrassed of his face. You told me everything, and I was monstrous to him."

"No, no." Mr. Bingley shook his head, giving her one of his wide smiles. "He is quite capable of bearing it, let me assure you. He is a proud man, I am afraid. He has been, all his life, told that he is superior and special, and now, this is all a blow to him. He cannot bear to be seen in that way."

Elizabeth was not sure that was all it was. Something in the turn of Mr. Darcy's phrase, the wryness with which he had spoken to her, she felt as if it went deeper than that, that something was very broken inside that man.

But she had to admit that Mr. Darcy was right.

Her primary emotion when it came to him now *was* pity.

She could see how a man might not wish to be regarded so. Perhaps that *was* pride, but she didn't blame him for it.

"It is good that you spoke to him," said Mr. Bingley. "We shall try again. I shall convince him to come out into company again, perhaps not at a ball, though, perhaps… I don't know. You and your sisters could advise me. Would there be interest in a whist party?"

"Oh, I think so," said Elizabeth. "But would that be any easier for Mr. Darcy, sitting at a table so near with others?"

"Perhaps not." Bingley sighed. "I shall think on it, then. Will you help me?"

"I would be glad to," said Elizabeth. "I feel, if I had not been so hard on him just now, that perhaps he might not have run away."

"I promise you, you were not in the wrong,' said Bingley. "But I should be glad of your help just the same."

CHAPTER TWO

Several days after the assembly, the ladies of Longbourn waited on those of Netherfield. The visit was quite well received by Mrs. Bennet, Elizabeth's mother, who was all agog over the prospect of Mr. Bingley and her eldest daughter, Jane.

Mrs. Bennet took all the credit for Jane's beauty, as if she had designed it herself and had a hand it making it come to be. Because of this, she had spent years now, since Jane came of age at about fifteen, throwing her eldest daughter in the way of rich and powerful men, sure that one of them must be carried away by Jane's beauty.

It is a truth universally acknowledged that all men become a bit of a beast when in the presence of an extraordinarily pretty girl. They cannot help but want to possess her, no matter how prudent it may or may not be.

Mrs. Bennet intended to take full advantage of these men's more primitive nature, and with Mr. Bingley, she was all but certain she had achieved it. He was quite enchanted with Jane, and Mrs. Bennet was like a preening cat, stretching and licking herself as she basked in the sun of the possible future.

Elizabeth, as always, found her mother entirely embarrassing. She could see that the ladies of Netherfield were losing patience with her mother's tendency to go on about Jane's virtues. Her beauty, her sweetness, her lovely singing voice. Her mother could not still her tongue.

In an attempt to quiet the woman, Elizabeth spoke up.

"Tell me, how does Mr. Darcy?"

" Oh, " said Miss Caroline Bingley. " Mr. Darcy. " Her voice had taken on a wistful quality.

"Now, now, Caroline," said her sister, Mrs. Hurst, "there is no need to muse overlong on Mr. Darcy."

" He was once such an eligible bachelor, " said Miss Bingley, her eyes wide and earnest. "You would not believe it, the change wrought in him. Why, he was so tall and so regal to look upon. The fineness of his features were unparalleled."

"Certainly a man is still the same man whether his face is scarred," said Elizabeth.

"One would think so, yes," said Miss Bingley, shaking her head, almost sorrowful.

" It is true that he is much changed," said Mrs. Hurst. "There used to be some mirth about him, but there is none now. He is quiet and sad."

" And angry. " Miss Bingley raised her head. " He was never angry before. He was never cruel. He was always quite kind to me, but as of late, the sharpness of his tongue, I do not care for it."

"There, now, Caroline, you are too sensitive," said Mrs. Hurst. "His injuries mean he is in constant pain."

" Truly? " said Elizabeth, leaning forward in her chair. "Pray, what happened to him?"

" A horrid carriage accident, or so I have heard," said Mrs. Hurst. " They were quite close to a cliff. Everything went over. It's a wonder anyone survived."

"When he used to look at me," said Miss Bingley, "there was something bright in his eyes, but it has been extinguished. He is quite a different man altogether. " She looked away, her face twisting, and Elizabeth saw the entire story of Miss Bingley's objections in an instant. She had fancied Mr. Darcy and thought he returned her affections, but now he was cold with her. She had a broken heart. Elizabeth felt for her. Miss Bingley was a bit haughty,

16

perhaps above her own station, but witnessing pain in others always brought out Elizabeth's sympathy. She did not like to witness anyone's suffering, even that of very wicked people.

"His sister did not survive," said Mrs. Hurst quietly. "He has never recovered from that. Miss Darcy, she was a lovely young girl. So pretty, so sweet, so talented."

"A voice like an angel," whispered Miss Bingley.

They were all quiet.

"Well," said Mrs. Bennet, "very sad for Mr. Darcy, to be sure, but he must learn to move on. Life is made for the living, as I always say. The dead are gone and bless them in heaven but those left behind must soldier on."

Mrs. Hurst and Miss Bingley gave her strained smiles.

"Losing someone so young is always very difficult," said Elizabeth.

"To be sure," agreed Jane. "I think Mr. Darcy must recover in his own time, in his own way."

"Spoken like the sweet girl you are," said Mrs. Bennet. "Why, did you know that when Jane was only sixteen years old, there was a gentlemen who came to town and fell madly in love with her and wrote such fine verses about her sweetness and goodness and beauty. She was quite lovely then, of course, but now, I think she is dazzling. Your brother seems to agree."

Miss Bingley put down her tea cup into its saucer with a clatter. "I say, Louisa, how long have we been here? Do we not have pressing business soon? That matter of which we spoke?"

"Oh, yes." Mrs. Hurst nodded sagely. "That matter. That very pressing matter."

"We must take our leave," said Miss Bingley. "We are so dreadfully sorry."

* * *

The days passed. The Bennet women paid a visit to Netherfield and were politely greeted by the sisters there, but neither Mr. Bingley nor Mr. Darcy was seen. They did not speak of him again. Perhaps it would have been considered rude to do so when he was so close by.

There was a dinner at Sir William Lucas's, and Mr. Bingley and his sisters were there, but Mr. Darcy did not attend. Elizabeth was a bit disappointed in that.

She found herself thinking about the man more and more. She wondered about the nature of his injuries, the constant pain he found himself in. She was not sure what she felt about it. A strange curiosity or an overwhelming flood of pity or something else entirely.

Since speaking to him, she had been compelled to reread *Much Ado About Nothing*. It was one of her favorites, mostly for the scenes between Benedick and Beatrice. She found the sparring nature of their conversations delightful.

She wondered if Mr. Darcy liked to read, and if so, if he only read proper things like poetry and plays from hundreds of years ago, or if he read novels as well. She herself read it all. She had quite gone through the library of Longbourn and would buy or borrow books wherever and whenever she could. It was one of her chief passions in life. Her mother, who was not much for reading, tended to look down upon it, but Elizabeth could not take her mother seriously. She was, in many ways, quite ridiculous, to Elizabeth's chagrin.

A week after the Meryton assembly, a request came from Miss Bingley and Mrs. Hurst, inviting Jane to dine at Netherfield. Mrs. Bennet was beside herself in glee about this development, and she conspired to send Jane on horseback in the rain, so that Jane would catch a cold and be obliged to stay overnight at Netherfield.

It all came to pass exactly as Mrs. Bennet had desired, and she was quite pleased. Mr. Bennet, Elizabeth's father, made some arch comment about how Mrs. Bennet should not be quite so proud of herself if her daughter did not recover.

"People do not die of trifling colds," said Mrs. Bennet, not the least bit concerned.

But Elizabeth herself began to become concerned. It was not so much that she thought Jane might die. She knew it was not quite so dire. But she began to worry about her sister, all alone in a strange house with strange people and feeling poorly. So, she made up her mind that she would go to Netherfield herself the following morning.

Her family tried to talk her out of it, but Elizabeth was insistent, and as she was no horsewoman, she decided to walk.

The walk itself proved muddy and long, and when Elizabeth arrived at Netherfield, her boots were rather dirty and the edges of her skirts had not escaped the mud either.

When she was shown into the breakfast parlor, the eyes of both Miss Bingley and Mrs. Hurst widened and they looked almost scandalized.

"You walked?" said Mrs. Hurst.

"In this weather?" said Miss Bingley.

"All alone?" said Mrs. Hurst. "Why, Mr. Hurst, can you believe it?"

"It has happened," said Mr. Hurst. "It must be so." He returned his attention to his breakfast.

"Well, I think it is lovely to see you, Miss Elizabeth," said Mr. Bingley, giving her a smile of true good humor and pleasure in her company.

"It was quite a long way to walk alone," came the voice of Mr. Darcy. He was sitting at the table, leaning back in his chair, and looking her over. "I daresay that if a woman did such a thing in London, her reputation might never survive."

"What?" said Elizabeth, giving him a pointed look.

"I suppose it's different here," said Darcy.

"It is," said Elizabeth. "There was nothing between here and there except cows and woods and grass. Nothing to threaten anyone's reputation."

" Indeed, well, when there is not much to threaten, " muttered Miss Bingley.

"Caroline," said Mrs. Hurst sharply.

Elizabeth pressed her lips together.

" Come now, Miss Bennet came yesterday by herself, " said Mr. Bingley. "There was none of this talk then."

"I think the walk agrees with your complexion," said Mr. Darcy. " Perhaps it is the high color of your cheeks, Miss Elizabeth. One look at you and my mind wanders in directions it ought not."

Miss Bingley drew herself up, horrified. " Why, Mr. Darcy, what a thing to say."

Mr. Darcy's scarred face twisted into the semblance of a smile. "Miss Bingley, I doubt you would exert yourself so."

"Indeed, I would not," said Miss Bingley.

Mr. Darcy's gaze burned into Elizabeth's. "I can't say I object to... exertions."

Now, Elizabeth's face was hot. What was he about? Why would he say such things to her? Why did she feel even warmer than she had from the exercise?

"Darcy," said Mr. Bingley, giving his friend a hard look. "What has gotten into you?"

" I rather got the impression Miss Elizabeth would not mind a bit of verbal sparring the last time I met her, " said Mr. Darcy, lifting his tea cup.

"If I offended you then, sir, I am sorry," said Elizabeth. " In truth, I thought that I had apologized before, but perhaps I did not make myself clear. If so, please accept my apologies now. I must make it quite plain that what I said to you was badly done. I repent of it. I hope we can forgive each other and not retaliate?"

Mr. Darcy laughed, but it was a funny laugh. He drank his tea, gazing at her over the cup.

She did not like the way he was looking at her. "I only came to see my sister. Perhaps if a servant could be spared to take me to her?"

"Of course," said Mr. Bingley, getting to his feet. "In fact, I shall take you there myself."

"Farewell, Miss Elizabeth," said Mr. Darcy.

Elizabeth felt hot all over. She refused to look at him, and she did not at all like the way that Miss Bingley was glaring at her.

"Come," said Mr. Bingley, nodding at her. "Let us go and visit your sister now."

"Yes," said Elizabeth, and she followed him.

When they were in the hallway, out of earshot, Mr. Bingley gave her an apologetic look. "I can't apologize enough for Mr. Darcy. He would never have said such things before the accident, but I'm afraid he has no ability to still his tongue these days. He says what he thinks. If it's any consolation, I think it means he likes you."

Elizabeth let out a disbelieving laugh. "He has an odd way of showing it."

"Truly," agreed Mr. Bingley. "And you mustn't mind Caroline, but I am afraid she has rather carried a torch for him for too long. It was always one-sided. Darcy has never shown her a bit of true interest, but he was kind enough to her on account of not wishing to embarrass her. Now, he has no scruples, and he has hurt her more than once. I have spoken to him about it. He does not listen. If he were not my dear friend, I would pack him off home. In truth, he has become rather a beast of a man."

"It is all right, Mr. Bingley. I have heard from your sister a bit of what he has been through. She says he is in near constant pain?"

"Yes," said Bingley. "He fears dependency on laudanum, however, and will not take a drop of it, so he suffers. I think that makes his tongue sharper too."

"I meant what I said about helping him," said Elizabeth. "Perhaps, if it is as you say, if he does truly like me, then that will be helpful."

Mr. Bingley smiled at her, all astonishment. "Oh, Miss

Elizabeth, between you and your sister, I am quite overcome. You are both the pinnacle of good manners and kindness. I would not blame you for abandoning any attempt to assist Mr. Darcy, especially after what he has said to you. But you do not do so, and it is to your credit. Your sister is also thus. I am astounded by the character of both of you."

"Thank you, Mr. Bingley, you are too kind."

"Here we are then." Mr. Bingley paused outside a door. He rapped on it gently. "Miss Bennet? Are you awake?"

"Mr. Bingley?" Jane called.

He pushed the door open. "You won't believe who's here."

"Oh, Lizzy!" cried Jane.

Elizabeth hurried across the room to embrace her sister on the bed. "I could not leave you alone, could I? How are you?"

"I am glad to see you," said Jane, gratitude written all over her expression.

Elizabeth knew she had done right in coming. Jane had been all alone here, and with only Mr. Bingley to be good to her. Everyone else in the house was rather dreadful.

* * *

It seemed that Elizabeth had made an enemy of Caroline Bingley, probably because of Mr. Darcy commenting on her appearance the way he had. Though it had been a slight, it had also been indicative of Mr. Darcy's being affected by the sight of Elizabeth.

Miss Bingley was jealous.

Around three o'clock, Elizabeth felt she must go, and Miss Bingley seemed happy of it, insisting Elizabeth take the carriage. When Jane seemed quite upset to see Elizabeth go, Mrs. Hurst said that Elizabeth must stay.

And then Mr. Bingley's sisters engaged in a rather tense conversation which lasted a bit too long, Miss Bingley being insistent that Elizabeth must go, and Mrs. Hurst telling Miss Bingley that sending her off would be rude.

22

Eventually, Miss Bingley caved to her sister's way of thinking and professed to Elizabeth in a very flat voice that she would not hear of Elizabeth going, that she must stay at Netherfield, of course. And then, before Elizabeth could respond, Miss Bingley swept out of the room.

Elizabeth agreed to stay, but only for Jane's sake. She needed to be there for her sister, but she did not find anything about staying at Netherfield particularly welcome. Her things were sent for from home, and she dressed for dinner with dread, not looking forward to seeing either Mr. Darcy or Miss Bingley.

By some miracle, neither were there.

Miss Bingley had cried off, complaining of a headache. Mr. Darcy was similarly afflicted by pain of some sort. Jane was not well enough to come down, being feverish.

It was only Elizabeth, Mr. Bingley, and the Hursts, then.

Mrs. Hurst was solicitous, trying to give excuses for her sister's behavior. "She must have been suffering from that headache earlier and dealing with the pain in silence. I can think of no other reason for her lack of politeness."

"I am not in any distress, Mrs. Hurst," said Elizabeth, cutting her meat into tiny pieces. "Pray do not trouble yourself further. We may leave the subject."

"It is Mr. Darcy," said Mrs. Hurst. "He distresses her." She turned to her brother. "I think you must say something to him, Charles."

"You think I have not said something? Indeed, a great many somethings?" Mr. Bingley shook his head. "He is not inclined to listen to me, I'm afraid."

"Well, then perhaps he ought to leave," said Mrs. Hurst. She turned to her husband. "Don't you think, so, dearest?"

"Oh, yes, quite," said Mr. Hurst, fitting a large bite of potato into his mouth and chewing.

"Not yet, Louisa," said Bingley. "We cannot turn our backs upon him."

"But he is different, Charles," said Mrs. Hurst. "You

know what it is they say of him, don't you?"

"That is utter hogwash," said Mr. Bingley. He shook his head. "We both know him, Louisa. He is not a murderer."

"Well, no one has seen that Mr. Wickham since," said Mrs. Hurst. "He is very likely dead."

"He fell over the cliff with the rest of them," said Mr. Bingley. "You can't blame Mr. Darcy for Wickham's demise."

"People do blame him! Anyway, I don't understand why Wickham was there, anyway. Was he in the carriage with Mr. Darcy and his sister? It's all highly irregular."

"He was a close friend in Mr. Darcy's boyhood, as I understand it, a friend of the family. It is not irregular at all that he was with them."

Mrs. Hurst huffed. "Well, it's not what people say."

Mr. Bingley looked pointedly at Elizabeth, who pretended to be very interested in her food. "I think, Louisa, that we had better find a different topic of conversation."

Mrs. Hurst turned to her plate, poking various things with her fork, and said nothing.

It was quiet for some time.

Mr. Bingley turned to Elizabeth. "I do hope your sister is comfortable?"

"I think so, sir," said Elizabeth. "As comfortable as possible, anyway. You have been quite a gracious host."

"She should stay as long as she needs," said Bingley. "Indeed, both of you should."

"Thank you," said Elizabeth.

Another long silence.

"I say," said Mrs. Hurst brightly. "The weather we've been having, is it quite typical for this part of the country?"

"Indeed," said Elizabeth, who thought that the weather of Hertfordshire could not differ overmuch from the weather of London. But it was rather more pleasant to speak of trifles than to be silent, so she launched into a detailed discourse on the weather patterns of November, which Mrs.

Hurst attended to with grave solemnity, asking questions here and there as if in an attempt to be sure she understood it perfectly.

And thus, the dinner passed.

CHAPTER THREE

Jane was being kept on her own wing in an attempt to minimize contagion, if there was any, so Elizabeth was obliged to walk back through the house on her own after she said goodnight to her sister.

She took a wrong turn at the end of the wing and somehow ended up on the wrong side of the house. Scolding herself, she found her way back to the main entranceway and was thus able to set herself right. Her father was always gently teasing her about her lack of direction. "Spending too much time thinking, Lizzy, and not enough paying attention to your surroundings," he would say.

It was true, of course. She did have a tendency to get lost in thought.

Currently, she was thinking of Jane, and whether or not she should hope for a match between her sister and Mr. Bingley. It was quiet obvious by now that Mr. Bingley was devoted to Jane, but marrying Mr. Bingley meant becoming attached to his relations as well. And the more gracious of the two sisters, Mrs. Hurst, was married and less likely to be about all the time. Instead, Jane would be forced to share meals and leisure time with Miss Bingley, who was not exactly enjoyable company.

Of course, Elizabeth thought, Miss Bingley would eventually get married, and then she would not be present as much. In truth, it was the man who mattered more than his family. Yes, she supposed it would be prudent for Jane to marry. And besides, if necessary, she could spend time with Jane and Bingley after their marriage and draw the ire of Miss Bingley, who did seem to dislike Elizabeth more than she looked down upon Jane.

Elizabeth found the stairs and began to ascend.

But, looking up, she found that someone else was descending the steps. He looked up at her, and it was Mr. Darcy.

She had to school herself to keep from wincing at the sight of his face. It looked so painful. He had been dreadfully injured in that fall indeed.

"Miss Bennet," said Mr. Darcy, the unscarred half of his mouth quirking upward, a half smile. "Wandering alone in the house at night, I see?"

"I'm afraid that after I said goodnight to my sister, I made a wrong turn and got a bit lost," she said. "But I am on the right track now. Good evening, sir." She started to ascend again.

His hand shot out and caught her by the arm, stopping her movement.

She gasped, startled. Had he touched her?

He wasn't touching her now. He looked startled, too, as if he had moved against his own volition. "I apologize, madam," he said in a low voice. "I did not mean to cause you any distress."

She gathered herself up. "I am quite all right, I assure you, only tired." She could not help but think of what Louisa had said at dinner, that a man had been in the carriage with them and that his body had never been found, that people said he had murdered the man. Regarding Mr. Darcy, she found it wasn't difficult to imagine him doing such a thing.

"Are you quite a reader of Shakespeare, then?" said Darcy's voice.

She licked her lips. "I beg your pardon?"

"When we met, you recognized *Much Ado About Nothing* straightaway. Do you read much of Shakespeare?"

"I have read his work," said Elizabeth. "Sometimes, the language is a bit difficult to decipher, but it is worth it if one uses one's mind to puzzle it out. And you, sir? Do you also enjoy Shakespeare?"

"I admit that I am more partial to the tragedies than the comedies," said Darcy.

"Yes, of course." She nodded. The comedies, with their boisterousness and happy endings, dual couples at the altar smiling and living happily ever after, she could see how he might not favor them what with the state of his life. "I, too, enjoy the tragedies. How could one not?"

"What is your favorite?"

"I couldn't say," she said. "I was once quite partial to *Macbeth*, but I find *Othello* quite affecting. Iago is chilling."

"Yes, indeed," said Darcy. "Quite an unsettling play, is it not?"

"I find it hard to believe that anyone could be so evil," said Elizabeth. "Surely, it is only a construction of such plays, a stock character, not found in real life. After all, in *Much Ado About Nothing*, we have Don John, who is much the same."

"Ah, yes, the machiavel," said Darcy. "An invention of fiction, you think?"

"It must be. No one is evil for the sake of evil," said Elizabeth. "No one enjoys such things."

"But isn't the broad path that leads to destruction broad precisely because so many walk upon it? If evil were not pleasurable, it would not be tempting, would it?"

"Yes, but that is different," said Elizabeth. "The pleasures of the flesh are tempting, but the way that Iago ruins Othello, delights in violence and death, that is something else entirely." And then she realized she had just said 'pleasures of the flesh' aloud in the presence of a man. It was a phrase spoken from the pulpit, to be sure, but it wasn't the sort of thing that a young lady spoke of so casually in polite society. She flushed. Why, Mr. Darcy would be thinking his earlier assessment of her was true, that she was improper, that her reputation was suspect.

Mr. Darcy was gazing at her, his dark eyes glittering. "Is it different, though? Perhaps Othello gives in too easily. Perhaps he tips over that edge because there is something that rises in him at the thought of climbing into his wife's bed and wrapping his hands tight around her creamy, bare neck."

Elizabeth shivered, strange sensations going through her. Mr. Darcy's voice was deep and rich, and it seemed to reach inside her and curl around her insides, making her feel off-kilter. What he was speaking off was horrid, though, and a tendril of fear crawled up her spine at the same time. She wanted to get away from him. She spoke, and her voice had gotten dreadfully thin. "I... I must be getting to bed, sir. I find I am quite tired."

"Of course," said Mr. Darcy, inclining his head. " I apologize for keeping you. I wish I shared your good opinion of humanity, in truth. I would like to believe there are not evil people among us. Would like to believe it very much."

She swallowed. "I don't suppose that is what I mean, not exactly. Surely, people do evil things, it is only that I don't think they delight in it."

He raised his eyebrows.

Suddenly, it was important that she got her idea across, even though she still felt unsettled by this man. "Look, for example, at dueling. When men go and shoot each other, it is not because they delight in spilling blood, because something rises in them at the thought of it. It is done out of anger and pride and a misplaced sense of honor. Some thought that there is some mystical sense of justice that will guide the bullet to kill the right man, but such things are preposterous."

"Well, there we agree," said Darcy. "Duels are not about justice. There is no justice in the world."

She licked her lips. "Perhaps not in the natural world. Perhaps that world is brutish and indifferent, but amongst the world of man, there is at least a chance for justice. Everything is not as bad as you seem to think it is, Mr. Darcy."

He laughed, surprised. "Oh, is that so?"

"Yes."

" And what is it that I should find favorable in my lot now, Miss Bennet?"

She cleared her throat. "Well... I am not saying you have not been through terrible loss, sir, and I don't mean to belittle that, I am sorry. But you are alive, are you not, and you are a man of some means, and you have a future ahead of you. Ruminating on the worst things in life will only serve to do yourself further injury."

"I see." He nodded, his half-smile wider but colder. "I shall simply put a happy face on it all, pretend that nothing is wrong."

"That is not what I meant," said Elizabeth.

"Of course not."

"That is, I do not know what it is like for you, and I can only imagine, which I may do poorly, but I think that misery is always there, if one wants to find it. It takes strength to rise above it, to see the good in the world, and I... well, if there is anything I can tell about you, sir, it is that you are strong."

He gazed at her, the smile sliding away from his face. He swallowed, and his Adam's apple bobbed, and there was suddenly something so... physical and male about him. She was aware that they were standing close to each other—too close—and she had a funny thought about reaching out and tracing the rope of the scar tissue on his face, gently sliding her forefinger over it.

She drew in a shuddering breath.

Mr. Darcy looked away. His voice was even deeper now, almost unsteady. "I have kept you far too long, madam. You have said you are tired. You must go to bed now."

"Yes," she said. "I am sure that I must."

"Good night."

"Good night." She fairly ran up the rest of the stairs. When she got back to her room, she undressed without calling for the maid that Mr. Bingley had designated for her use, because she could not bear being in the presence of another person.

She was not sure what she felt about Mr. Darcy.

Fear, she told herself firmly. *He is a most unpleasant man.*

That statement about Othello, for instance, that was disturbing.

Yes, she allowed, it had been disturbing. And yet...

No, she would not allow herself to finish that thought. It was preposterous to even entertain it.

* * *

Darcy pushed open the door and found Bingley standing by the fire, a glass of brandy in one hand. He looked up when the door opened, eyes raised.

" Yes, I am sorry I am late, " said Darcy, going straightaway to pour himself a glass of brandy as well. " I met Miss Bennet in the hallway—that is Miss Elizabeth Bennet—and we had a conversation that got away from us."

"What do you mean?"

"I don't know, it just went on too long." Darcy settled down in a chair in front of the fire, sipping at his drink. "What is it you wanted to say to me?"

Bingley sat down in a chair next to him. "Well, I don't know where to start."

"Perhaps I can say it for you," said Darcy, gazing into the flames. " You find my lack of manners unacceptable. Your sister Caroline is in some distress, and it is my doing. You are not at all pleased by the way that I conduct myself, and you want me to pack up and go in the morning, leave you all in peace."

"Oh, Darcy, I'm not sending you away."

31

"You should," said Darcy, slumping down in the chair. "I am only going to behave worse else."

Bingley shot him an annoyed glance. "You are doing it on purpose, because you want me to send you away."

Darcy sipped his drink and neither confirmed nor denied this.

"If you want to leave, leave." Bingley gestured vaguely in the direction of the road.

"If I leave on my own, you will pester me with more letters," said Darcy. "You will likely beg me to come with you to London for the Season. You will—"

"Darcy would I have rented this house in the country if I intended to be in London for the winter?"

"Perhaps," said Darcy.

"Listen, I am worried about you, that is all. It's not good for you to be alone. It wasn't good for you to have spent your entire period of mourning by yourself, drunk all the time."

"I was in pain. The drink helps a bit." He took a gulp of brandy. It burned its way into his belly.

"That does not mean it was good for you."

"You and Miss Elizabeth are the same," said Mr. Darcy. "You both wish me to leave my misery behind and try to find something to be happy about."

"She said that to you?" said Bingley.

"She's a very sharp-tongued sort of girl," said Mr. Darcy, running his finger around the rim of his glass. "She has very particular ideas, and she's not afraid of making sure you know what she means. She has no qualms about being openly disagreeable."

"I say, are we talking about the same girl? She is as sweet as her elder sister. Every time I have interacted with her, she has been nothing but decorum personified."

Darcy smirked.

"You provoke her," said Bingley.

"Yes," Darcy said softly. He took another gulp of brandy.

"I suppose I do. I think I enjoy provoking her more than I have enjoyed anything since ... " And he could not bring himself to utter the words 'Georgiana's death' aloud.

"Hmm," said Bingley, looking him over. "Well, that's interesting. I thought you might have objections to the family."

Darcy squinted at him. " The family? What are you talking about?"

"The Bennet family."

" Oh, indeed. I suppose they must have a family. Everyone does, after all." Then he laughed hollowly. "Oh, wait, in fact, *I* do not have a family."

"Darcy..." Bingley sighed.

"What does the father do?"

" He is a gentleman," said Bingley. " He has an estate, rather smaller than Netherfield. Quite a bit smaller than Pemberley."

Darcy drank more brandy.

"Oh, come, man," said Bingley. "You are not yourself at all. Why, when I was entranced by that girl in Derbyshire, you had a list of reasons as long as your arm that I should leave off her. You are always putting your nose into my business like a... like your aunt, Lady Catherine."

" Oh, that was cruel. " Darcy grimaced, but he didn't actually sound very upset. "Take that back."

"For heaven's sake, what do you think of Miss Bennet?"

"I thought I had just explained that she was disagreeable, but that I found the sight of her countenance rose-colored from a walk in the open air rather... stirring."

"Oh, Darcy, no, the eldest Miss Bennet."

"I think nothing of her," said Darcy, finishing his drink. "I have never conversed with her, I don't think. She is pretty, I suppose, but quiet."

"I am in love with her."

"Truly?" Darcy squinted at Bingley.

" Truly, " said Bingley. " You have no objections to the

match?"

"Match? You're going to marry her?"

"I think so, yes."

" Well, if that's what you want." Darcy shrugged. " I suppose if you get married, you'll be distracted, and you'll stop treating me as your project."

"Perhaps *you* should get married," said Bingley.

"To whom?" Darcy chuckled.

"Darcy, your body may be damaged, but your fortune is not, and neither is your ability to get heirs. There is nothing wrong with you, and there are great many women who would not care—"

"Who would close their eyes against the sight of my face moving over them?" said Darcy. "No, thank you."

"I imagine what you're speaking of is often done in the dark," said Bingley. " But you needn't be vulgar. There is quite a bit more to marriage, you know."

" Well, I suppose you and Miss Bennet will be discovering that shortly." Darcy looked down at his glass. "I seem to have drunk all my drink, so I'll need to refill it if you want to have a congratulatory toast."

"Honestly, Darcy, you can't be so vain—"

"It's not vanity," Darcy snapped.

Bingley raised his eyebrows.

Darcy sighed, sitting up straight in his chair. " Bingley, there was a time in my life when I could manage it. I could go to the balls and dance with women and have ridiculous mindless conversations about nothing. But now, I don't care about any of it. I don't care at all. And they are so... so silly and pretty and delicate. I would ... putting my hands on them, it would soil them. I am not for those sorts of women anymore."

"Oh?" said Bingley in a knowing tone. " And perhaps a disagreeable woman, one who can't seem to stop speaking her mind, that is who you are for?"

Darcy let out a funny noise. He looked into the fire, and

he was overcome for a moment. "I couldn't do that to her. Miss Elizabeth is… she's quite stunning in her way. No, no. She must have someone better than me. I am bitter and broken."

"You're going to have to marry someone."

"Why?"

"To carry on the line, of course. You can't simply let the Darcy name die out."

"Well, it's not as if I don't have cousins." Darcy tried to get up, and pain shot up his leg. He grunted. "I say, Bingley, would you be so good as to fill my glass again?"

"You shouldn't drink so much," said Bingley.

"Fill my glass or consent for me to leave," said Darcy, glaring at his friend. "I won't have you scolding me. You are an old woman."

"I will scold as much as I please." But Bingley snatched the glass away and got to his feet.

CHAPTER FOUR

The following day, Mrs. Bennet came to call at Netherfield with the other three Bennet sisters in tow. Lydia and Kitty babbled quite a lot at the beginning, commenting upon everything they saw, from the size of the drawing room to the chandeliers to the biscuits served with tea.

Elizabeth found herself trying in vain to shush them. She did not mind that they were obviously annoying Miss Bingley. Elizabeth did not care about her opinion. However, she wanted to remain in Mr. Bingley's good graces. Indeed, if her sisters and her mother did not stop with their rather embarrassing displays, Mr. Bingley might be frightened away from the family and would not continue his pursuit of Jane.

Try as Elizabeth might, she could not manage to direct the conversation elsewhere or to convince her sisters to keep their mouths shut. It did not help that Mrs. Bennet encouraged them, agreeing with nearly everything they said.

Mr. Bingley, however, was most polite. He seemed not the least bit concerned over the chattering of her sisters. In fact, Elizabeth thought he might be a bit amused, almost charmed. Lord, he was perfect for Jane, wasn't he?

" And you, Mr. Bingley, how do you like it here at Netherfield?" asked Mrs. Bennet.

" Exceedingly well, madam, " said Bingley, smiling. " I must say the company in this part of the country is first rate."

"Well, it's always a bit of a roll of the dice in the country, is it not?" came a dark, sardonic voice.

Everyone turned as Mr. Darcy made his way into the sitting room. He had a cane that morning, and Elizabeth had not seen him with it. He moved forward with it, his scars illuminated in the light through the windows, and Elizabeth had to admit he resembled some kind of grotesque three-legged beast. She schooled herself not to allow this to show on her face, however, coolly regarding Mr. Darcy as he approached.

Her mother, however, was so startled that she choked on a biscuit and was afflicted by an attack of coughing.

Mr. Darcy settled down on a chair, looking at those assembled. "After all, there are simply less people about in the country. One might settle somewhere in which the company is agreeable, but one might chance into a group of quite horrid people instead."

Mrs. Bennet furrowed her brow, quite offended. "Why, what a thing to say!"

"I'm sorry," said Mr. Bingley in a tight voice, glaring at Mr. Darcy. "I'm afraid I have not introduced Mr. Darcy. May I present him to you? And this, Mr. Darcy, is Mrs. Bennet, and her daughters, Miss Lydia, Miss Catherine, and Miss Mary."

"Charmed, I'm sure," said Mr. Darcy, helping himself to a biscuit.

"I'm sorry," said Mrs. Bennet, still quite aflutter, "but I simply can't let stand the idea that there are horrid people about in the country. Why certainly, there are horrid people everywhere, and most especially in the city. The city is quite rife with crime, is it not?"

"No, madam," said Elizabeth, shaking her head at her mother. "You misunderstand him. He does not mean that all people in the country are horrid, or that there are no horrid people in the city."

"No, of course not," said Darcy. "But in the city, if one manages to make the acquaintance of a horrid group of

37

people, one can avoid them, being that the society is so varied. In the country, one must often dine and socialize with the same families over and over. If one makes an unfortunate acquaintance, one must bear it."

"Darcy, truly, it is not quite so easily to steer clear of certain people in the city, either," said Bingley. "I did not realize you would be coming down this morning. Your valet said you were quite out of sorts."

"Yes, I've made a remarkable recovery." Darcy's mouth was full of biscuit. Crumbs dribbled onto his cravat as he chewed.

Mrs. Bennet was aghast.

Bingley bowed his head, and his face was turning red.

Darcy swallowed and brushed at the crumbs.

"Well," said Mrs. Bennet, "if anyone would flourish in the city, I think it would be my Jane, who is so very lovely that no one can help but love her. I often tell my other girls that they are nothing to her. They are so very plain when compared to her beauty."

"You tell your daughters they are plain?" said Mr. Darcy, reaching for another biscuit. "Tell me, how do they respond to such pronouncements?"

"It is simply a fact, Mr. Darcy," said Mrs. Bennet. "Why, it has nothing to do with how amiable one is. After all, we are quite close with the Lucas girls. Their Charlotte is practically my sixth daughter, so often is she with us. And she is so very plain, but we do not mind in the least. She is a lovely girl."

"If you do not mind," said Mr. Darcy, "then what is the advantage in pointing it out at all?"

"Oh, I don't," said Mrs. Bennet. "That is, I would never say to Charlotte's face that she was plain. That would be rather rude."

"I see." Mr. Darcy nodded. "Then it is only something to be said when she cannot hear, unless of course, the subjects are your own daughters, because rudeness does not apply to family."

Elizabeth was torn between wanting to slap Mr. Darcy in the face and rather wanting to hug him. She had not heard someone put her mother in her place so soundly in her entire life. Even her own father, who routinely disagreed with his wife, tended to do so in such a way that only fed his own amusement, not necessarily in a way that communicated his censure.

"No," said Mrs. Bennet. "Mr. Darcy, I believe you are willfully misunderstanding me."

"Oh," said Mr. Darcy, biting into his biscuit. "I did not realize."

Miss Bingley spoke up. "Perhaps Mrs. Bennet is growing tired after so long a visit. You have seen that your daughter is quite well cared for. I imagine that was the purpose of your errand."

"Oh, to be sure," said Mrs. Bennet. "I am so grateful for your keeping Jane here. She is quite ill, I think. She would not complain, of course, it is not her way. She has always been thus, even when she was a child. She is an exemplary daughter. Of course, she is my own, so perhaps I am blinded by my deep love for her, but I cannot but think my picture is accurate."

"Oh, I agree wholeheartedly," said Mr. Bingley. "She is an extraordinary creature, your daughter."

Miss Bingley tried to smile, but it didn't reach her eyes. "Well, I'm sure she'll be recovered soon and home with you."

"Nothing would bring you more joy than to be quit of her, Caroline," said Mr. Darcy, who was getting more crumbs on his cravat.

"Darcy!" exclaimed Bingley, on his feet.

"I assure you, that is not true," said Miss Bingley, also on her feet.

"You're a wretched liar, Miss Bingley," said Mr. Darcy. "And your manners leave something to be desired. Truly, if you can't pretend to be polite, why not be truthful about your scorn?"

"I'm afraid I need to be excused," said Miss Bingley. Her lower lip was trembling. "A headache has come upon me rather suddenly."

"Caroline," said Mr. Bingley. "Wait but a moment."

However, Miss Bingley had fled from the room.

Mr. Bingley pointed at Mr. Darcy. "I hope you're pleased with yourself."

Darcy shoved the rest of his biscuit in his mouth, and he did look rather pleased.

Mr. Bingley turned to Mrs. Bennet. " I truly cannot apologize enough, madam. Please, my friend has been through a recent tragedy, and I am afraid he is not himself."

Darcy raised his eyebrows, but he didn't contradict Mr. Bingley.

Mr. Bingley turned to the younger Bennet sisters. " I know what might cheer us all. Plans for a ball. What do you say? Ought I throw a ball here at Netherfield?"

"Oh, yes!" said Lydia, smiling widely. "A ball is quite the thing. We should like that very much."

" Then you shall name the day, " said Mr. Bingley. "Anytime after your sister is recovered."

* * *

Darcy stayed in the drawing room as they all left, eating biscuit after biscuit.

Moments later, Bingley returned to the room, walking briskly across the carpet to stand in front of him, arms crossed over his chest.

Darcy reached for another biscuit.

Bingley reached down and snatched it out of his hand.

Darcy furrowed his brow, disappointed. He sighed.

" I have determined that you don't actually want to leave," said Bingley.

"Oh, is that so?"

"If you wanted to leave, you would leave," said Bingley.

40

"I think you are behaving in this manner, because you are being a child. A very spoiled child. You are throwing a tantrum for attention."

Darcy sat up in his chair, leaning on his cane.

Bingley put his finger in Darcy's face. "Well, listen, Darcy, I don't care. Yes, it's all very horrible that you have a scarred face and that you are in constant pain, but I'm done with hearing about it."

"I'm sorry my discontent has ceased to amuse you."

"Oh, don't play that card," said Mr. Bingley. "It won't work with me. I am not indifferent to your pain. Indeed, I have made allowances for far too long because of it. I know you are in physical pain and emotional pain and that you have become mean and improper and awful. But you will stop."

"How do you propose to make me do that?"

"I shall throw you out else."

"Excellent, well, then I shall be gone before dinner."

"Will you really?" Bingley tilted his chin. "I don't think you will. I think you want to stay. I think you want to feel better. I think you are being a child and you only need a firm hand. So, listen, Fitzwilliam, here is what you will do. You will apologize first to Miss Bingley, and then we shall go round to the Bennet household, and you will apologize there. Sincere apologies, mind you, nothing rote and unconvincing. And from now on, if you can't think of something nice to say, you will keep your mouth shut. Am I clear?"

"I shall tell my valet to start packing."

"We shall see if that is what you do," said Bingley and stalked out of the room.

* * *

Darcy didn't leave. He made up his mind to go, but he never gave any orders to his valet, and he never called for his carriage to be hooked up to horses, and he didn't send word along to Pemberley that he would be coming home.

Perhaps Bingley was right. Perhaps he didn't want to

leave. Maybe he even wanted to feel a bit of happiness.

He didn't deserve to feel happiness, of course, not when he was an utter failure, a worthless being.

But he didn't go anywhere.

And so, he found himself in a sitting room with Caroline Bingley, her brother looking on.

"I owe you an apology," said Mr. Darcy.

Miss Bingley would not meet his gaze. Or perhaps she could not bear to look at his ugly face. Either way, he pushed on.

Mr. Darcy cleared his throat. "Perhaps I owe you many apologies, Miss Bingley. I suppose I should have explained earlier to you that I was not attracted to you in return."

She looked up at him, her eyes wide.

He licked his lips. "I know that you could no longer find anything about me attractive, so don't concern yourself with thinking I consider your interest in me to be ongoing."

"Mr. Darcy... it is not your face that has made me feel badly toward you," Miss Bingley murmured. "It is only the manner in which you now speak to me. Indeed to everyone. You were always so polite before."

"I was awkward before," said Mr. Darcy. "I had trouble speaking to everyone. I thought all the things I am saying aloud now, but I held my tongue out of consideration."

"You thought these things?"

"Darcy," said Bingley. "Is this an apology? Because it does not quite sound like one."

"I thought I was being polite, but I was concealing the truth, and it caused you further pain when it was revealed," said Darcy. "I am sorry that I caused you pain. In truth, it does not bring me any pleasure to think that I have hurt you, Miss Bingley. I wish you well. I wish you happiness, in fact. I am deeply sorry for anything that I have done which has made your happiness difficult to attain."

"Oh," said Miss Bingley, nodding. "Well, I thank you for your frankness, sir, and for your apology."

"I promise not to be so unthoughtful in the future," he said.

"You are forgiven," said Miss Bingley.

"I do not deserve that," said Mr. Darcy. He turned to Bingley, eyebrows raised, a silent question. Had he done that well enough?

Bingley looked annoyed, but he nodded.

Bingley still insisted that Mr. Darcy apologize to the Bennets, but was willing to let the matter rest for a bit.

So, time passed, and Miss Jane Bennet soon felt well enough to return home. She and Miss Elizabeth left and were conducted home. Mr. Darcy had no occasion to speak to either of them, even though he rather supposed he owed Elizabeth some sort of apology as well, if only for his rudeness to her mother.

But he had to admit he disliked Elizabeth's mother. She was an artless woman who considered herself crafty, even though everyone could see through her. There was nothing more detestable.

Poor Elizabeth, he thought, growing up with that woman telling her that she was plain, that she was nothing compared to her sister. She was not a plain woman, not at all. She had a lively look to her, a pleasing countenance, eyes that were bright with intelligence, a body both slim and round in the right places... Perhaps he had given too much time to thinking about the beauty of Elizabeth Bennet, but she was very beautiful.

She was beautiful and smart and willful and stubborn, and he was overcome by his feelings toward her.

Perhaps that was why he stayed. In Pemberley, there was no chance of seeing her or of hearing her speak.

Eventually, Bingley was making plans for the ball at Netherfield, and he thought that a visit to the Bennets was just the thing for both an invitation and for Mr. Darcy to beg Mrs. Bennet's pardon.

Darcy wasn't keen on it, but he did it.

He bowed low and told Mrs. Bennet that he was dreadfully sorry for what he had said to her. He said that he had been in an awful accident that had left him permanently injured and that the pain put him in a frightful mood much of the time. This was no excuse for his poor behavior, however, and he could not find any reason why he should have said the things he said. Indeed, there was no reason for Mrs. Bennet to forgive him at all. He had been wretched. He had no right to beg for her pardon, but he did it anyway. He appealed to her better nature to give him that which he did not deserve.

Mrs. Bennet seemed to enjoy his turn of speech and told him to forget all of it before launching into a long speech about how lovely Jane's hair looked glinting in the sunlight.

Darcy gazed across the room at Elizabeth, who was sitting by the fire, a book closed in her lap. She locked eyes with him, and he felt fire in her gaze, his body coming undone.

If he could bear the idea of saddling a woman with his disfigured body and spirit for a lifetime, he would ask Elizabeth Bennet to marry him. He had grown to understand a few things about the family's situation.

There were five girls, no male heir, and judging from the size and state of their house, there couldn't be nearly enough money to support them all. Yes, Mrs. Bennet was nearly desperate to marry off her daughters. It didn't excuse her behavior, but perhaps she was so blinded by fear of the future that she could not behave in a prudent manner.

No, they needed the money, and an offer from him, above their station, Elizabeth would say yes. Of course she would. She would feel as though she had no choice. He wouldn't put her in that position. A woman such as her would surely attract another man, a better man, one who might make her smile.

He liked the way she smiled.

But as she looked at him then, there was no gaiety about

her at all.

Still, she did not look away.

Neither did he.

CHAPTER FIVE

Elizabeth wished she could stop thinking about Mr. Darcy, but it didn't seem possible. He seemed to haunt her thoughts, even her dreams. She'd dreamed one night that Mr. Darcy was Iago, whispering in her ear that she must strangle Jane and take Mr. Bingley for herself.

She awoke in a sweat, horrified by the dream. She was not the least bit interested in Mr. Bingley and she would cut off her own arm rather than hurt Jane.

This was what Mr. Darcy wrought within her—horrors and pain. She did not wish to think of him at all. Every thought she had of him was unfavorable. But she did wonder at the fact that she could not drive him from her head.

She would not call it temptation, not as they had spoken of in the stairwell. Instead, she might term it torment. Whatever the case, it would not fade, and it would not go away.

She wished he would leave. She knew that the ball at Netherfield loomed, and she did not wish to see him there. She would be quite happy if he left and went back to wherever it was that he had come from.

But whenever she expressed these thoughts aloud, Jane would admonish her gently that Mr. Darcy had been through so much sadness that surely they must make allowances for him.

And Elizabeth would feel a stab of guilt, for she did feel pity for the man. She didn't like to see anyone in pain, and she would not wish more of it on Mr. Darcy.

If only he had not looked at her the way that he had, at the end of their conversation in the stairwell. It was that look that haunted her, sneaked up and assaulted her when she wasn't expecting it. No one had ever looked at her that way before. She didn't even know what the look meant, but whenever she thought about it, her entire body seemed to get shivery and taut, and it was most distracting.

She wished for something—*anything*—to occupy her mind except for Mr. Darcy.

And then Mr. Collins arrived, and she regretted her wish.

Mr. Collins was a heavy looking man of about five and twenty. He had a roundish face, and his nose was too long for it, giving him an odd look, rather a warring sense of seriousness and levity.

Upon arriving, he was quick to say that he had come "prepared to admire" the Bennet sisters, although he did not wish to be forward or to say more.

The meaning was clear.

He was looking for a wife amongst the Bennet girls. Mrs. Bennet was overjoyed. After all, this would solve most of her problems. The house would remain in the family, and her own daughter would not turn her out, nor turn out the other girls. Everything would be quite tidy in that way.

But Mr. Collins was a horror. He was quite the most awful man she had ever met, worse than Mr. Darcy in some way that she could not quite explain. Indeed, the men were nothing alike, not at all, so it was difficult to quantify why Mr. Collins disgusted her so.

He was a boor, and he was stupid.

She could point out all manner of disagreeable things about Mr. Darcy, but she could never call him stupid. He had a razor sharp wit, and he was unafraid of using it.

But Mr. Collins, he seemed unaware of the subtleties of conversation about him. He was a man with no imagination, and she could not marry him.

However, it seemed rather clear that Mr. Collins intended to ask for her hand. At first, he must have been interested in Jane, but he'd been turned from that path, likely because of Jane's attachment to Mr. Bingley, and Elizabeth was the next oldest daughter. It all made sense in light of that.

It became abundantly clear when she had a conversation with Mr. Collins about dancing, and he expressed his belief that dancing was good and proper and even biblical. Did not King David, the man after God's own heart, dance in the streets of Jerusalem? Was there not a 'time to dance' as put forth by Solomon's Ecclesiastes? In light of all that, Mr. Collins wished to dance with all of his cousins.

"And, dear Miss Elizabeth, if I could have the honor of your hand for the first two dances, it would please me greatly."

The first two dances?

Lord.

He was intent, then. He would ask for Elizabeth's hand. The only question would be when. Certainly not at the ball, she thought. It was not a place for securing an engagement. She should have that long in order to think of some plan to escape marrying Collins.

She could *not* marry him.

No, it was out of the question.

* * *

The first hour of the Netherfield Ball was taken up by the dances with the odious Mr. Collins, who was a worse dancer than he was a conversationalist, if such a thing could be believed. He moved stiffly through the first two dances, often performing the steps wrong without realizing it, and apologizing twice for coming far too close to her. Once his hand touched the bare part of her arm, above her gloves.

Revulsion cut through her, and she had a brief moment of imagining a kiss between her and Mr. Collins, and she thought she might be ill.

She was relieved when she was released by him and she fled to a corner of the room to hide. At least that was done. Mr. Collins couldn't ask for another dance, not without declaring to the entire world that they were engaged. Three dances together simply wasn't done. He would wait to ask for her hand instead of asking for another dance, she was sure of it.

Of course, she had not thought of any way to escape marrying Collins.

She had tried, but she had no recourse. If she refused him, her mother would never forgive her. And what of her sisters, what of them? Perhaps if Jane did marry Bingley, it would all turn out all right in the end, and perhaps...

She turned and realized that she was not in this corner alone.

Mr. Darcy was leaning on his cane, his gaze so dark and heavy she thought she could feel it on her flesh.

"Mr. Darcy!" she exclaimed.

"Miss Bennet," he said. "I suppose I have not apologized to you."

Ah, yes, she remembered his apology to her mother, but she had thought he had skirted the edge of being ironic with that. The exaggerated nature of it all, it had been a bit too much to be truly sincere. "Spare me an apology you do not mean, sir."

"Why would you say such a thing?"

"I do not believe that you are ever sorry," she said.

"Now, that is not true," said Mr. Darcy. "I must make mistakes, must I not? I am a mortal man, like anyone else. It only follows that I should need to apologize from time to time."

"Rather more often than that, I should think, judging from the time I have spent with you."

He laughed.

She winced. "Oh, it is I who must apologize, I'm afraid. You do bring out something within me, sir. When I am near you, I am not my best self."

"There is a better side to you, then?" said Mr. Darcy. "That I can hardly believe. You are rather exquisite. I cannot dream of any improvements I would make. No, you are perfect quite the way you are."

Elizabeth's breath caught in her throat at the compliment. "What are you saying, sir? I had rather the impression that you did not..." She shifted on her feet. "That is, I thought it was mutually agreed that we were not overly fond of the other." And then she cringed again, because that was still too bald to say aloud.

He stepped closer, leaning on his cane, his dark eyes glittering. "You are mistaken, Miss Bennet. This lack of fondness you speak of, it is only on your side."

She sighed. "Then I suppose I must apologize again."

"No, indeed not. I am not an easy man to like. I realize this." He nodded across the room at Mr. Collins. "You have the attentions of that gentleman, I see. The first two dances. Not that he seems particularly skilled at dancing."

Elizabeth shuddered. "Oh, don't look at him. He might notice us over here." She turned away, as if she could blend into the surroundings.

Mr. Darcy was quiet.

She looked up at him.

"Am I to understand you are not desirous of that man's attentions?"

Elizabeth did not answer. She gazed at Mr. Darcy and wondered how it was that he would say that she was perfect. She thought of the way he had apologized to her mother, how there had been a tinge of sarcasm in everything he said, and she knew that had been absent from his compliment of her.

But this man had been awful to her. He had cast aspersions on her reputation. He had challenged everything she said to him. He had been rude and ugly and cruel. She did not like this man.

50

And yet, he was looking at her in that way again, that way that no one had ever looked at her, and she found herself beginning to speak, words spilling and tumbling from her lips as if she could not stop them.

* * *

She was talking, and Darcy was watching her lips, which were lovely and perfectly shaped.

"You see, my father's estate is entailed upon Mr. Collins, and he is here to try to find a bride," said Elizabeth. "If he does so, it will be nice and tidy for the family. We will have no worries after my father dies, and we shall all be looked after properly. I think he would have asked Jane, but my mother thinks that Jane will become engaged to Mr. Bingley by and by, and it is such a good match, she would not ruin it. So, she turned him off her, and so now, Mr. Collins has set his sights on me, and I… oh, I don't know…" She wrung her hands. "I know what the proper thing to do would be, what I should do for my family, but I don't know if I can do it."

"Marry him?" said Mr. Darcy, looking across the room at Mr. Collins, a chill going through his body.

"It is what I should do," said Elizabeth.

Darcy shook his head. It was one thing to swear off pursuing Elizabeth Bennet in theory. It was quite another to watch her be paired off right in front of his nose. And to be paired off with… with that.

He had not spoken to Mr. Collins, so perhaps he was being uncharitable. His lone observation of him had been his dancing with Elizabeth, and he had been far from proficient at dancing. It was perhaps unfair of Darcy to judge a man on his dance steps, but Darcy thought it spoke to a lack of any interest in doing this right. If one was going to dance, one put in the time to understand *how* to dance.

Mr. Collins clearly had not done that. He had a look about him, something vaguely ridiculous, and Mr. Darcy didn't like him.

He might not have liked any man that had danced the

first two dances of the night with Elizabeth, however, he had to admit.

He could have put it down to simply jealousy, but now... now Elizabeth was telling him that she didn't like Mr. Collins and that she didn't wish to marry him, and now...

He drew in a sharp breath through his nose.

" I suppose he is a proper enough sort of gentleman, " Elizabeth said faintly. "I would marry him and go to Rosings, where he is the parson."

"Rosings?" said Darcy absently. "That is where my aunt Lady Catherine resides."

" Lady Catherine is your aunt? " Elizabeth seemed surprised by this.

" Yes," he said, and he wasn't looking at her. He was looking across the room at the back of Mr. Collins's head, and he was thinking about how he could not watch Elizabeth married to that man. He could not do it.

" I would be able to leave home, be mistress of my own house," said Elizabeth. "However, I get the idea that I might not be, in truth. Mr. Collins has spent a great deal of time talking about how Lady Catherine has dictated various aspects of his life, from putting shelves in closets to what he has for tea, and I rather think that I would be expected to do exactly as she says." Elizabeth bit down on her bottom lip. "I'm not very good with doing as I'm told, I'm afraid."

Darcy looked at her. "No, I can see that. You shouldn't."

"Shouldn't what?"

He cleared his throat. "Forgive me, I'm not sure what it is that I'm saying." He needed to be careful here. He couldn' t blurt out a proposal to her, not now. Or couldn't he? He was a wretched man, scarred both inside and out, but if he married her now, wouldn't he be rescuing her?

" If I turn him down, I don't know what he might do," said Elizabeth. "He might be so angry that he will turn us all out when he inherits Longbourn. He might be quite offended. And if I turn him down, I think my mother will murder me. She will be so very angry."

" Listen, Miss Bennet, perhaps I could be of some assistance. " He had means. If she was worried about her family, about her mother — as dreadful as the woman was — Darcy could see to it that they were all taken care of — in style — forever. He could solve all her problems. She would consent to it, wouldn't she?

She looked up at him, and he saw the barest flinch when her gaze slid over his scars. "What do you mean, Mr. Darcy? How could you possibly help?"

" Ah ... " He swallowed. She wouldn't consent. How could she? He was an abomination. She could not look upon his face without being horrified. He looked down at his feet.

"Mr. Darcy?"

He looked back up. " Oh, he seems to be coming this way."

Elizabeth turned. " He spotted me. He did say that he wanted to stick closely to me all evening." She grimaced.

"Would you like to dance, Miss Bennet?" said Mr. Darcy.

She turned back to him, eyes wide in surprise.

"He can't stick close to you if you're dancing with me."

" True, " said Elizabeth. She seemed to force herself to smile. "Yes, thank you, Mr. Darcy. I will dance with you."

Of course, she didn't have much choice, did she? Refusing to dance with him would mean that she must refuse to dance with anyone. He had not done her much of a favor at all. She did not like him.

* * *

Darcy bowed to Elizabeth, his leg pulsing painfully at him. He had left behind his cane, of course. It would not do to have it with him when he was trying to dance. But his injuries had given him worse trouble than usual as of late, perhaps owing to the succession of rain the previous week.

He pressed his lips into a grim line and waited for the music to begin.

When it did, he was gratified to learn that the dancing

53

seemed to stir within him a physical memory. His body knew what to do, and it seemed that movement was loosening the tight muscles in his leg. It felt almost good.

So, thoughts of the pain fled from his head, and he watched Elizabeth's face, and he began to think rather perverse thoughts.

Elizabeth did not like him, that much was plain. She had been quite clear when she said that she was not fond of him.

Elizabeth also did not like Mr. Collins. She had made that plain as well. But Elizabeth could not refuse Mr. Collins. She had no choice but to accept him. It was what her family expected of her, and she must do her duty.

So, in this instance, it was not a question of whether or not Elizabeth could have a happy life married to a man she cared for. Instead, it was the punishing existence of marrying Mr. Collins and dealing with the inexorable force that was his aunt or marrying Mr. Darcy.

Neither would please Elizabeth, of course, but Mr. Darcy thought that a marriage to him was preferable.

"It is a very nice arrangement, do you not think?" said Elizabeth in a tight voice. "This version of the music that the musicians have chosen?"

"Oh, yes, quite," said Mr. Darcy without paying much mind to her.

If he proposed to her, she might come to the same conclusion as he did, or she might deny him, simply out of a backhanded horror at the thought of being tied to a man like him.

If, instead, he took the choice out of her hands, then he would improve her life, and the life of her family, and he would have her for himself.

It was a monstrous thought.

But there were monstrous thoughts within him now and monstrous actions too. What had happened on that cliff, with Georgiana, with Wickham, it had changed him. He was capable of things he had never thought possible, this he knew.

" I say, Mr. Darcy, I have commented on the dance, perhaps you might say something?"

"Say something?" he echoed. "What would you like me to say?"

" Oh, I don ' t know. Anything. Perhaps you might comment on the room or the number of dancers or the light fixtures. *Anything.*"

" Certainly. Perhaps you might assume that I have said whatever it is that pleases you and respond accordingly."

" Oh, that is … " She glared at him. " Are you always thus?"

"You know that I am," he said.

"You are disagreeable."

"Very much," he said.

"You cannot be polite to save your life."

"No, I daresay I cannot."

" And you have no shame or regret about such things either. You have no concern about anyone but yourself, and I try to tell myself this is because you are in pain, but, upon my word, Mr. Darcy, it is becoming a rather thin excuse." Color was rising in her cheeks, and it made her all the more lovely.

He moved before he could really think of what it was he was doing. Certainly, he had mused over this course of action only seconds before, but he had not committed to the action, and yet, now, here it was, happening, and he knew he should stop himself.

He didn't stop.

He abandoned the dance altogether, stepping close to her, so that there were mere inches between their bodies. He brought up his hand and he slid his fingers over her jaw.

She gasped.

He was touching her, touching her skin, touching her face, and he had no right to do so.

"Mr. Darcy —"

"Peace," he said in a low, awful voice. "I will stop your mouth."

And then he was kissing her.

In the middle of the dance floor.

In front of everyone.

CHAPTER SIX

The minute he pulled away, he regretted it.

The kiss itself had been rather lovely. Elizabeth had been stunned but eager somehow. Her hands had gone to his shoulders and dug into his skin, and her mouth had opened to allow access of his tongue, and he had swept against her once. Then twice.

She had whimpered against him, her fingers painfully going into his flesh.

And then he had some presence of mind and let go.

Her expression was so shocked and horrified that he hated himself.

She stepped back, both of her gloved hands going to cover her mouth, her eyes so wide it looked painful. Even through her hands, a noise tore its way out of her throat, a noise of panic and dread.

He cringed. What had he done? "Miss Bennet, I..." He swallowed. "I should not have—"

But she wasn't listening to him. She had turned and she was walking away from him now, going as quickly as she could. She nearly tripped on her skirts, so she gathered them up with one hand, and then she ran.

She rushed from the room.

Everyone gazed after her.

It was utterly silent now, he realized. The music had stopped. The dancing had stopped. Everything had stopped. Everyone was staring at him.

He was a bit used to that, because people tended to stare

now. They could not look away from the horror that was his face.

He knew that wasn't why they were staring. At least, it wasn't the only reason why they were staring.

He bowed his head. Pain surged up his leg, through his thigh, into his hip. Damnation, where was his cane?

Another moment and he staggered off in search of it.

Immediately, the room erupted in the buzz of low conversation.

Darcy limped across the room, gritting his teeth, until he had the cane in his hand. He turned around, and there was Bingley and also another gentleman. Darcy had seen him before, but he wasn't really sure who he was. He thought he had been introduced...

Oh, yes.

That was Mr. Bennet, Elizabeth's father.

Lovely.

Mr. Bennet didn't look quite as angry as a wronged father could look. He didn't look angry at all. His face seemed frozen in a state of horrified bewilderment, as if he had not the wherewithal to even comprehend what had just occurred.

He kept coming at Darcy, closer and closer.

Bingley reached out and caught the man by the shoulder. "Mr. Bennet!" He sounded out of breath.

Mr. Bennet turned to Mr. Bingley, gazing at the other man as if he did not know who he was.

"He wants to marry her," said Mr. Bingley, who then turned to Darcy for confirmation. "Isn't that right, Darcy?"

"Indeed," said Darcy. "That is, in fact, why I..." He shook his head. "You must excuse me, I did not mean to do what I just did. I did it without thinking. It seemed as if something dreadful came over me." He cleared his throat. "Should someone go after Miss Elizabeth to see if she is all right?"

"I'm sure her mother or sisters can do that," said Bingley.

"By heaven, Darcy, I don't know who you are anymore."

"No," said Darcy. "I'm not sure I do either."

Mr. Bennet looked down at his cravat as if he did not even know what a cravat was. Then he looked up at Darcy. "You say you wish to marry my daughter."

"I do," said Darcy. "Very much."

"If that is what you wished, sir, I must say I wonder why you did not simply ask her, instead of behaving like a barbarian." Mr. Bennet's eyes flashed.

"I... I really don't know," said Darcy.

"No, I see that you don't," said Mr. Bennet. He pointed at him. "You don't know my daughter."

"Sir, on numerous occasions I have—"

"You know nothing of her. She is not the sort of girl who can be forced into things. My Lizzy, she is..." Mr. Bennet's face twisted. "You don't know her."

"No, you are right," said Darcy, the realization of it all like a gaping hole in his stomach. Elizabeth would not stand for what he had done to her. "I have wronged her. I have taken horrid advantage of her." And ruined her, he realized. If she wouldn't marry him after this, she would never be married at all.

"Would that you could have realized that several moments ago," said Mr. Bennet.

"Indeed," said Darcy in a whisper.

"I don't like you," said Mr. Bennet, looking Darcy over. "I don't like you at all. And I'll be damned if I let you hurt my Lizzy. Do you understand me? I am her father. I will protect her. No matter what the cost."

* * *

Elizabeth gasped for air. She was halfway to the end of the Netherfield drive when Jane caught up with her, huddled into her coat.

Elizabeth was only in her evening gown, the cold wind biting into her bare upper arms and her neck. She didn't mind. The cold was good.

"Lizzy," said Jane. "Where are you going?"

"I don't know." Elizabeth shook her head, and she was afraid that now that Jane was here, that someone was showing her kindness, she might burst into tears.

No, she wouldn't cry. She had just now been thrust into a world in which all choice had been stripped from her, and she had no control of anything, but she could keep herself from crying.

"Why did he do it?" said Jane.

"I don't know," said Elizabeth. "I had no sense that he would do anything of that nature."

"Did he say anything to you beforehand?"

"I was insulting him, telling him that he had better stop behaving so badly," said Elizabeth. "Do you suppose he did it for revenge, to teach me a lesson? It seems a rather hard thing to do in response. I was not any harsher on him than I had been before, I don't think."

"I have no sense of it," said Jane. "You know him much better than me. I have barely exchanged three words with him."

"He made some comment about my reputation before. Perhaps he thought I was… perhaps his opinion of me was so low, he thought me ruined already."

"Oh, Lizzy, I am so dreadfully sorry." Jane threw her arms around her sister.

"Everyone will think…" Elizabeth let Jane hug her, but she could not embrace her in return. "What if Mr. Bingley no longer wants to be associated with us because of this? They will say such dreadful things about me. They will say that I encouraged him in some way, and I swear I did not."

"Mr. Bingley knows what Mr. Darcy is like. I am sure he will lay the blame where it deserves," said Jane. She pulled back. "Well, perhaps Mr. Darcy will marry you."

"Oh," said Elizabeth dully. For some reason, this outcome had not occurred to her.

"Would you marry him?"

Marry him. Kiss him again. Have him tell her again in a velvet voice that she was perfect.

Her lips parted. "Oh," she said again, her voice barely audible.

* * *

After that, the ball was basically over. There was no more dancing, just clusters of people talking amongst themselves. Elizabeth saw them when she was ushered through the rooms to find her mother, who was silent and quiet and huddled on a chair, tears leaking out of her eyes.

Elizabeth did not think she'd ever seen her mother thus.

By the time they had all been herded into the carriage, her mother had rallied. She was talking again, her voice shrill. "Mr. Bennet, you must make that man marry Lizzy."

Lizzy's father had not spoken at all. He was like a beaten man. He would not look at anyone, not at his wife or his daughters.

"Mr. Bennet, can you hear me?" said Mrs. Bennet. "I am right next to you, so I can't see how it would be possible that you did not hear me. Look at me, I tell you. Look at me this instant."

Nothing from Mr. Bennet.

The carriage lurched to movement, heading back toward home, to Longbourn.

"We are all ruined else," said Mrs. Bennet. Then she squinted. "Lord, what has become of Mr. Collins? He came along with us in the carriage, didn't he?"

"I don't know, Mama," said Jane in a low voice. "I did not think to collect him I'm afraid."

"Oh, dear," said Mrs. Bennet. "Do you think we ought to go back for him? He is our guest. But he must be mortified. He intended to ask Lizzy for her hand and now ... oh. He would never marry her now. He could not. He would not marry any of our daughters now."

"I think that I saw him with the Lucases," said Mary.

"Oh." Mrs. Bennet sat up straight. "Well, isn't that just

like Lady Lucas, snatching him away and parading her daughters before him. And I must say, Lizzy is not quite so plain as the Lucas girls, but how could she tempt him now? Lord. Oh, *Lord*, Mr. Bennet, what are you going to do about this?"

Mr. Bennet raised his gaze finally. "Quiet, Fanny."

Mrs. Bennet huffed. "Mr. Bennet?"

" You needn't worry about Mr. Darcy. He is quite desirous of Lizzy's hand. But I shall not force her to marry a man that she despises."

Mrs. Bennet sputtered. "What? If he will have her, then we are spared. How could you possibly — "

"He trespassed upon our daughter's virtue against her will," said Mr. Bennet sharply. "That is not the sort of man I want for a son-in-law."

* * *

Later, Elizabeth was in her father's study. It was late, but no one had gone to bed for the night. Everyone was far too on edge to know what to do.

Word had come from the Lucases that Mr. Collins would be staying there for the night, and the servant bringing it had asked for some fresh clothes for Mr. Collins to bring back for the morrow.

The younger girls, Lydia and Kitty, seemed excited about it all, unable to stop their chattering. Mary was dour as always. Mrs. Bennet was in a fury against her husband. Jane was trying to soothe everyone.

And so escaping to her father's study was a blessing.

"I meant what I said." Her father's voice cut through the quiet. She had just been adjusting to the fact that she was shut away from her noisy family. The quiet was welcome. Now, she struggled to attend to her father.

She blinked at him. She could not speak. It was odd. She had the strangest sensation as though she was moving through the world without actually touching anything. She could tell that she was sitting on a chair, but she could not quite feel it, as though her skin was numb.

"I won't force you to take that awful man," said Mr. Bennet.

"But Papa..." Elizabeth furrowed her brow. "That will reflect badly on the entire family."

"I don't care," said her father. "You need not suffer because of that man's behavior. He had no right to do what he did. Anyone could see that you had not encouraged him in any way. And indeed, even if you had, there is no call for that sort of brutishness. He is a rich man, used to getting whatever it is he wants, and he wants you. Well, you are my daughter, and I won't roll over and give you to him."

Elizabeth licked her lips. "I-I think I have to marry him, Papa."

"You do not. I am telling you, you do not."

"If I do not marry him, the reputation of the entire family will be called into question," said Elizabeth. "Jane may not be able to marry Mr. Bingley. He may not wish to sully his name by tying himself to us. And the other girls, all of them, they will never find husbands, and I shall surely never have a husband. If he will marry me, Papa, I think I must do it."

Her father shook his head at her. "Did you encourage this man?"

"No."

"Do you wish to marry him?"

"I..." She swallowed. "My future if I do not marry him is to live out the rest of my days in this house with my miserable sisters and my angry mother, who will never forgive me. I think being the mistress of my own home might be preferable."

"Yes, but to be tied to that Darcy!"

"Well, I am sure his house is bigger than ours. Perhaps I won't have to see him too often." She swallowed hard.

"Lizzy, I can't let you do this."

"I don't see as I have much choice," she said softly.

CHAPTER SEVEN

Elizabeth had listened outside the door to the conversation between her father and Mr. Darcy, but if she had expected to hear some kind of argument between them, she had been disappointed. They had done their business quickly, speaking in clipped and precise tones, perfectly polite.

It was all settled then. She was to be married and with all haste.

When Mr. Darcy came out of her father's study, Elizabeth stole down the hallway.

Mr. Darcy was speaking as he walked down the hallway. She could hear his cane clicking against the floor. "I should like to speak to Miss Elizabeth if I might," he said, and then he rounded the corner more quickly than she could have anticipated. "Oh," he said.

For he could see her. She had not had the time to hide herself. She nodded at him, giving him a brief curtsy. "Sir."

He inclined his head. "Would you walk with me?"

"Of course," she said.

"Take Jane with you," said her father from behind Mr. Darcy.

"What does it matter now, Papa?" said Elizabeth, shrugging. "I have no reputation to protect anymore."

Mr. Darcy's jaw tightened. He looked down.

So, he was ashamed of himself. She didn't care. It did nothing to excuse him.

They went out into the garden to walk.

They were quiet for some time. She was certainly not going to begin any kind of conversation with him. He wanted this audience with her. He could speak.

By and by, he did. His voice was halting. "I thought I should ... try to explain myself. What I did, I gave no previous sign that I would do it. You must wonder at my motivations."

"You thought to embarrass me," she said. "And then you felt guilty, so you made an offer for my hand."

"Indeed, it wasn't that way at all. The truth is that I keenly love and admire you. You are, indeed, quite different from other women."

"Oh," said Elizabeth. "I see. So, you don't in fact like women?"

He was flummoxed. "What?"

"You intend to compliment me by saying that I am unlike the other members of my sex? I *am* a woman. How is it at all complimentary to be told I am not *like* a woman?"

He cleared his throat. "I only meant that you are unique in a pleasing way. To me. I am quite enchanted by you, and I always have been. But I realize you dislike me."

"Well, I do now."

"You told me, in fact, before our dance that you did."

"I did not mean..." She cocked her head to one side. She took him in, his scarred face, his dark and expressive eyes, his broad shoulders. Why was she doing this? Her father had told her that she needn't do it, and she knew he would have fixed it for her somehow. But it was the same as before, when she could not stop thinking of him, even though all the thoughts were monstrous thoughts. She was drawn to him in some perverse, awful way. She did not seem capable of staying away from him.

She had to admit, she would like it if he kissed her again.

"I knew that you would not consent to marry me if I asked," he said.

"So, you took my choice away from me."

"Yes." He nodded. "It was wrong of me, I know. Amongst my sins, it is perhaps the most evil thing I have done. I reasoned that your choices were to be unhappy with that boor Collins or unhappy with me. I thought that I might be able to provide you with a more comfortable life, and I... well, I *want* you, Miss Elizabeth. Badly. So... I did what I did, but I confess that if I could, I would go back in time and take it back, for I would have you not to hate me, and I know that I have secured your ire for all eternity."

She just gaped at him, his words reverberating through her. *I want you. Badly.* She didn't really understand why they affected her. What did she care what Mr. Darcy wanted? He was a man for which she felt alternate shades of pity and revulsion, that was all.

But there was the fact that she had consented to be his wife.

No, she did not wish to think on any of that. She shoved all of it aside and lifted her chin. "You have indeed, sir. I loathe you, and I always will."

* * *

"Have I done the right thing, Jane?" Elizabeth's voice was a whisper in the darkness. She lay in bed next to her sister, and she did not even know if Jane was awake, let alone whether she would answer.

"Lizzy?" came Jane's voice. She shifted in bed, rolling onto her side, and yawned. "What are you saying? Are you awake or talking in your sleep?"

Elizabeth picked at the covers over her chest. "Papa said I did not have to marry him."

"Papa is a dreamer, and we both know it," said Jane quietly.

Elizabeth turned to face Jane. "What do you mean?"

"Oh, Lizzy, I know you are his favorite, and that you worship him, but you must see it? He loves us, I know he does, but he has never seriously considered any future that was negative in any way, nor has he made any pains to prepare for one. He pokes fun at mother and the other girls and he holes up in his study. But for all his talk of how Mama will spend us out of house and home, he puts no regulations on the expenditures of the household, and he has saved nothing extra for us girls. He is… he means well, Lizzy, but he is overly optimistic about everything. You had no choice. You had to agree to marry Mr. Darcy."

Elizabeth swallowed a lump in her throat. "Yes."

"Surely you know that's the truth."

Elizabeth only breathed.

"I don't agree with it," said Jane, rolling onto her back. "It's horrid, that's what it is. Any man who wishes can force his lips on some woman, destroy her reputation, and force her to marry him. That's uncivilized, if you ask me. How could you have guarded your virtue against such an attack? You were innocent, and he is a monster."

"I don't think he meant it," Elizabeth said quietly.

"What do you mean? Of course he meant it."

"I don't think he thought it through," said Elizabeth. "I think it was done impulsively."

"Are you making excuses for him?"

"No, of course not."

Jane sighed. "I suppose it would be better if you could find a way to forgive him. He is going to be your husband, after all."

"Indeed, if anyone could forgive him, I thought it would be you, dear Jane. You are always seeing the best in everyone."

" Well, Mr. Darcy's best is buried somewhere deep inside," Jane muttered.

Elizabeth sighed.

"Look, there is no use being melancholy over it," said Jane. "You will be married to a man of means, and you will be able to use that money to secure your own comfort. That is perhaps a silver lining."

"I will send for you as soon as you can, if you'll come,"

said Elizabeth.

"Of course."

"Oh, but no." Elizabeth shook her head. "I would take you from Mr. Bingley."

"Oh, yes, I suppose I had not thought of that."

" Well, you and Mr. Bingley will be married soon enough," said Elizabeth.

"Lizzy, he has not asked me."

" But I think he will," said Elizabeth. " He adores you. Anyone with eyes can see so. Anyway, after you are married, I shall have Darcy invite you both to visit us. Bingley is his friend. He will consent to it."

"It sounds lovely," said Jane. "I hope it all comes to pass just as you envision it. And if Mr. Bingley does marry me, and you cannot invite us, I shall make Bingley invite the two of you."

" Yes, " said Elizabeth. " One way or the other, we will find a way to be together."

"I will write you until we are reunited," said Jane. "One letter a day, and you must do the same, whether you have gotten a response or not. In that way, it will be as though we are still together. We will know what is happening in each other's lives."

"Yes, I promise to write," said Elizabeth.

Jane sniffed.

"Jane, dear, are you crying?"

"No, Lizzy, I would not cry, of course I would not. These are happy plans we make."

The girls embraced in the darkness, and if their pillows were a bit wetter after, neither would own to it.

* * *

Mr. Darcy staggered across the room, leaning heavily on his cane. He was so intent on getting to his chair in front of the fire, he bypassed getting a drink entirely.

Bingley was standing by the fireplace. He turned, brow furrowed. "Darcy, let me help you."

"No," Darcy growled. His injuries were particularly painful that day, but he would not be assisted like an old man. He fell into the chair with a grunt, shutting his eyes.

"Are you all right?" said Bingley.

"No, I'm not all right," muttered Darcy. "The entire left side of my body is in agonies. I am a wretch who has ruined the life of a very nice young lady. I am very far from all right."

Bingley sighed.

"Oh, and you chastise my behavior, as well you should," said Darcy. "Why, I am a worm. I am an insect."

Bingley rolled his eyes. "Don't be melodramatic. I'll get you a drink."

"I would be most obliged."

Bingley poured some port into a glass and brought it to his friend. "Here."

Darcy took the glass and gulped at it, too eagerly, he knew. He grimaced, forcing himself to stop. Gritting his teeth, he stretched his injured leg toward the fire, thinking that the warmth might help it.

"I think you have misrepresented the extent of your injuries to me," said Bingley quietly.

"I have not," said Darcy. "It is only that it is worse some days than others. This cold wet in the air lately, it makes everything ache."

Bingley pushed a stool over to him. "Would you care to rest your leg on this?"

Darcy sighed. "I don't need you to fuss over me."

"Oh, for heaven's sake, we are friends. Accept the kindness and stop being such a curmudgeon."

Darcy set his leg on the stool. It was better. "Thank you." He drank more of his port.

Bingley sat down next to him.

For several long moments, they sat in silence, staring into the fire.

"What you said before, about my chastising you, I have

not, you know," said Bingley. "I have not uttered one word of censure for your actions. I feel you've done well enough at that on your own. Anyone can see you regret what you did. I don't blame you, Darcy."

"Well, who else is to blame?"

"I think you might blame yourself overmuch," said Bingley. "Whatever happened in the carriage accident—"

"I've asked you never to speak of that."

"It was an accident, Darcy. It was not your fault. If you keep thinking of yourself as someone who makes grave mistakes, it becomes a self-fulfilling prophecy. Give yourself the gift of a good opinion of yourself."

"Oh, stop it," said Darcy. "If I could will myself into good cheer, I would, I promise. I know that my problems are an inconvenience for you. I'll be married soon and out of the way."

"It really isn't about me, Darcy. I am your friend. I wish only the best for you."

Darcy finished the rest of the port. Between the alcohol and the fire, he felt the pains in his body starting to dim.

"You will write to me, won't you?" said Bingley. "Don't go off to Pemberley and disappear again."

"I never disappeared. I was there the entire time."

"I will write to you. You must promise to write back."

"Very well. I promise."

CHAPTER EIGHT

The wedding was held but three days hence, and despite the fact that it was a hastily organized event, it seemed that everyone in Hertfordshire was in attendance, probably because they had all seen the kiss at the ball, and now wanted to see the matter drawn to its proper conclusion.

The wedding breakfast was a boisterous affair, everyone talking and laughing and eating, wishing good health to the presumably happy couple.

Elizabeth discovered that Mr. Collins was engaged to Charlotte, and she could not believe her friend had decided to do such a thing. However, she was marrying Mr. Darcy, so perhaps she did not understand anything. She was not sure she understood herself.

Her new husband was starkly silent compared to the frivolity that surrounded them. He did not speak to her, and she did not speak to him either. But she was uncomfortably aware of him, as if he were a dark shadow at the edge of her eyesight, following her everywhere. She was inextricably tied to him now. What had she done?

By afternoon, they were off in a carriage, bound for his home of Pemberley.

They traveled into the evening and only stopped hours after night had fallen. Mr. Darcy traveled with his valet, but Elizabeth did not have a maid of her own, nor were any of the servants from Longbourn able to be spared to go along with her on the journey. Mr. Darcy had been concerned about this, but Elizabeth had assured him she was used to undressing and dressing herself on occasion. After all, with six women in the Bennet household and only a few servants to go round, it was only practical to acquire some of these skills herself.

Due to the number of rooms already taken in the inn, Mr. Darcy informed her they would need to share a room, which was only proper, she supposed, since it was technically their wedding night. But she could not help but feel apprehensive.

He ordered bread and stew brought to the room, and they sat at a table next to the fire and ate in silence.

When they were done, Elizabeth gazed at the bed in the room, trepidation filling her.

Mr. Darcy rang for someone to take away their dirty plates and bowls. When they were cleared, he shut the door behind the servant and turned to her. "It should go without saying that I would not expect any sort of consummation of these vows this evening, not after everything I have put you through."

Elizabeth's heart squeezed and relief coursed through her, hot and liquid. There was a tinge of something else mixed in, though. Disappointment? But that didn't make sense.

Her discussion with her mother the night before had relied heavily on a time that Elizabeth had come upon two horses rutting in the field, and her mother had explained it was much the same with people, that the man must mount the woman in order to put his seed into her. Elizabeth had been horrified, because whatever had been happening between those horses had not looked comfortable in the least.

And then her mother had added the tidbit of information that it could also be done facing one another, that it was usually done that way, and Elizabeth was even more confused. She pictured lying on her back in bed, Mr. Darcy mounting her as if there was a saddle on her and then... well, what happened after that?

Anyway, maybe she was curious. She must be

misunderstanding her mother in some way, and maybe she wanted to understand it all. Maybe that was the disappointment. That must be it.

She swallowed, looking at Mr. Darcy and feeling a jolt go through her when she did. She looked away immediately.

"We will have to share the bed," said Mr. Darcy, "but only to sleep, I assure you."

She licked her lips.

"Miss Benn—that is, Mrs. Darcy," he said. "Is this acceptable to you?"

"Yes, of course." She stood up.

Mr. Darcy nodded. "Very well, then. I shall retire to the room with my valet to undress and give you your privacy to do it alone. When you are finished, you extinguish the lamps and get into bed."

"Of course, sir," she said.

He left the room.

And that was when she realized that her dress had buttons going all up and down the back of it, and that it would be quite impossible for her to undo them on her own.

She tried.

She managed a few, at the top of her neck and at the base of her spine, but the ones in the middle, she could not reach.

After trying and failing to unbutton them for some time, wrenching her arm in a quite painful way, she gave up and sat down at the table to await Mr. Darcy's return.

He was gone for quite some time, nearly a half hour.

When he did return, he pushed the door open slowly, carrying a candle. He was quite surprised to see the lights still on and his new bride still dressed.

He was wearing only a loose shirt and his smalls, and the shirt he wore was open at his chest. She could see his skin, a hint of dark hair that grew there. Her body tightened against her will.

She stood up. "I could not reach my buttons, I'm afraid." She blushed. "Would you mind...?"

"Oh certainly," said Mr. Darcy, setting down the candle. "I should have realized."

"No, I should have," said Elizabeth. "I don't know why it slipped my mind." She turned around.

His fingers were warm and deft and strong. She shivered as they made quick work of her buttons.

"There," he said, and his voice had gotten quite deep.

"Finished?"

"Yes." His voice caught.

"Thank you." She turned around, starting to slide her dress off her shoulders.

He gazed at her, his dark eyes ravenous.

Her breath caught in her throat.

He shook himself. "My apologies, madam. I shall quit the room again—"

"It's all right," she said. "Simply turn your back, I suppose."

"Yes, that will do." He turned.

She peered at him from behind. His sleeping shirt was a little bit translucent. She could see the lines of his back through it. They were strong and firm. And then, at the base of his spine, one one side, more ropes of scar tissue. She looked away.

Quickly, she divested herself of her dress and climbed into the bed in her shift. "All right, you may turn around." Why was her voice so high pitched?

He did.

She picked up the lamp on the bedside table. "I'll turn this down."

"Yes," he said.

She did, and the room was now only lit by Mr. Darcy's candle. She watched as he carried it over to the bed, and all that was illuminated was the scarred side of his face.

She went rigid, waiting for that visage to join her in bed, feeling like an ancient woman sacrificed to a monstrous god so that crops would grow.

74

She drew in a shaky breath.

He climbed into the bed next to her and blew out the candle.

Darkness.

* * *

The next morning, Elizabeth woke to lovely warmth, and she snuggled into it, relishing the feeling. Jane was sometimes rather bad about pulling the covers off the bed in her sleep and Elizabeth often woke shivering. But this morning, she was toasty and perfect, so warm that she did not wish to get out of bed at all.

The warmth shifted, pressing into her, and her eyes fluttered open, because she had not expected movement.

That was when she realized that she was somehow in Mr. Darcy's arms. He was wrapped around her, and her face was pressed into his chest. Their legs were entangled.

She did not move. She was not sure how this had occurred. When they had gone to sleep the night before, they had been on opposite sides of the bed, not touching at all. Somehow, sleep had drawn them together, though, and she could not say it was unpleasant.

He sighed in his sleep, tightening one arm around her.

Her instinct was to get even closer, to rub herself against him like a satisfied cat.

Instead, she carefully extricated herself from Mr. Darcy and his body. She found her trunk and dressed in a simple morning dress and set about putting a few more logs on the fire, because it had burned down and had obviously not been attended by servants at the inn.

"What are you doing?" came a sleep ravaged voice.

She turned. "Nothing, just seeing to the fire."

"That's not your job," said Mr. Darcy, sitting up in bed. "You're Mrs. Darcy. You're my wife. We have people for that."

"Yes, I know, but we are at an inn, and there was nothing else to do so..." She clasped her hands in front of her.

Mr. Darcy grunted. He thrust his leg out of the bed and began to knead it above the knee, grimacing.

"Oh!" she said. "Are you in pain?"

"I'm always in pain," said Mr. Darcy. "Give me a moment and I will be able to go to my valet."

"Perhaps I should go and fetch him?" said Elizabeth.

"No, no," said Mr. Darcy, grimacing again, deeper, and then vaulting out of the bed. He hobbled across the room, yawning. He scratched his flat stomach through his shirt, and a dark thrill went through Elizabeth.

She twisted her fingers together.

"We'll be on our way as soon as possible," said Darcy. "I want to reach Pemberley in time for dinner."

Elizabeth turned away, her heart pattering inside her ribs. There was something about the way Mr. Darcy looked, something that was most unsettling. He was so damaged, yes — the scars, the limp — but then there was something else in the way he was shaped — his strength, his... oh, she did not know, his maleness? It was most... why, she could not say *appealing*, could she?

Lord, she remembered being in bed with him, pressed up against the solid warmth of his body and she flushed.

They did not pause long to break their fast, having only some tea, eggs, and toast before setting out into the cold morning. The air was quite cold indeed, hovering just above the temperature when everything would freeze, and it was drizzling rain. There was a white mist in the air and the sky was gray.

Mr. Darcy muttered to himself about the dreadfulness of the weather and the effect on his injuries. Once they were jostling along in the carriage, he shifted position often, contorting his face into frightful expressions, which were only made worse by his scarred visage.

He payed Elizabeth no mind, only seethed, and seemed even more beastlike the longer that they drove.

When they did arrive at Pemberley, it was late.

Because of the gray weather, darkness was approaching even earlier than usual, although this was the time of year when darkness encroached on the afternoon as it was.

Mr. Darcy pointed out Pemberley to her. " Your new home," he said in a rasping voice, the pain seeming to have robbed him of his ability to speak with strength.

At first, she could not make anything out. There was still a heavy mist over everything, and it seemed to have grown worse as night began to fall.

But then, she did see the house, high up on the hill.

Calling it a house was rather inaccurate. A castle was almost more like it. It had no turrets or towers, but it was massive, gray stone rising out of the mists and reaching for the heavens. It looked like something out of a book she might read, and in those sorts of books, whatever waited for the heroine in the high house on the hill was never good.

She tried to scold herself out of such a silly thought. She must keep up her spirits, after all. She would arrive and settle in and have some time before dinner to write her first letter to Jane.

How should she describe Pemberley to her sister?

I arrived today at the hall of the goblin king, she thought, trying to make a joke. But it did not make her feel like smiling. It twisted her insides into knots, and dread cut through her.

Darcy shifted position again, crying out sharply when he tried to move his leg.

"Sir, is there anything that I can do for—"

"Leave it," Darcy snarled, his eyes flashing.

She retreated into the back of the seat of the carriage. Goblin king, indeed.

The rest of the short journey she spent staring out the window at a row of twisting, gnarled trees, their limbs bare in the winter. They went all the way up and down the drive, and they seemed to close them in from the rest of the world, their dark branches still and skeletal.

Eventually, they arrived and Mr. Darcy could not make it out of the carriage on his own, so great was his pain.

His valet and the driver attempted to help, but Darcy growled at them to leave him alone and would not take their assistance.

Elizabeth stood outside the carriage, rain mixed with sleet and snow falling on her head, chilling her. Her nose was cold, and so were her fingers and toes.

It took nearly ten minutes, but eventually Darcy managed to stand on his own. Then he made his slow and painstaking way up the steps to the front door of Pemberley, putting nearly all his weight on his cane. With each step, he growled in pain.

Elizabeth trailed behind him, now soaked and frozen.

She hoped that it would be warm inside, but it was not.

The massive doors opened onto a great room with a massive fire place, but the fire did not seem to bring any heat to the room. There were three large dogs lying in front of the fire, their tongues hanging out.

A plump woman scampered down the staircase, which stretched upward to the higher levels of the house. She was wringing her hands. " Mr. Darcy! Can you not send word when you are coming home?"

Darcy looked up at her, his nostrils flaring. "Is that Lady there by the fire? " He lifted his cane and pointed in the direction of the dogs.

Snow was swirling in from outside. Mr. Darcy's valet shut the door. "Mrs. Peters, I did send on a letter. Must have gotten lost between there and here," said the valet.

Darcy put his cane down and moved deliberately across the floor toward the dogs. His cane echoed in the massive room every time it touched the ground. "I believe it is Lady. Yes, I am quite sure." He poked the dog with his cane.

" Mr. Darcy! " Elizabeth couldn't help but exclaiming. There was no call to be cruel to a dog.

Now Mr. Darcy was close to the fire, and the flames stained his face and cravat red and orange. The light danced a reflection in his dark eyes. "I told you I wanted another home found for that dog!" he roared.

Mrs. Peters was at the bottom of the steps. She scurried over to Mr. Darcy. "Now, now, we didn't know you were coming, did we?" She bent down and caught the dog by the collar. She tugged. The dog resisted.

"Mrs. Peters," said the valet. "Come away from there. You do not have the strength to fight that dog."

Mr. Darcy was trembling. His teeth were bared. "So, you only hide her from me when I am in residence, is that how it is? I want someone else to care for that dog. I have made my position on this matter quite plain, and to have it completely ignored is vexing." Spit was flying from his mouth. He was in quite a state.

Elizabeth backed away, even though she was not anywhere near him. He was frightful. What was the matter with him?

Mrs. Peters gave another tug on the dog's collar. "Now, if you please, it is not the dog's fault who owned her. She never asked for that, did she? She and the others are littermates. It seems a great cruelty to separate them when they've all grown up—"

"I want that dog out of here!" Darcy cried. "I will have nothing of his in my house."

Mrs. Peters shrank from him.

"Sir," said the valet, who was now standing behind Mrs. Peters. "Perhaps we should get you upstairs, settled near a fire with a drink? Wouldn't that be better? The staff was not expecting you. Give them time to do something with the dog."

"I daresay it's snow and ice out there," said Mrs. Peters. "You wouldn't turn a poor beast out into the cold, would you?"

Mr. Darcy slammed his cane on the floor. "I believe I

have already answered that question."

"The dog is not Georgie, sir, and Georgie himself left her behind all those years ago!" protested Mrs. Peters.

"Get rid of her," said Mr. Darcy in a low voice, and he nodded at his valet. "A drink, yes. I would have a drink."

"Come, sir," said the valet, offering Darcy his arm.

Darcy glowered at it, and then seemed to crumple into the other man. Together, they made their way slowly to the steps and began to ascend.

"Oh," said Mrs. Peters, looking after them. "Oh, dear, dear, dear." Then she seemed to notice Elizabeth for the first time. "Oh, excuse me. What have we here?"

Elizabeth smoothed her skirts. "Hello. I'm Mr. Darcy's wife."

Mrs. Peter's eyes widened. "Indeed?"

Elizabeth nodded.

"Wife, you say?" Mrs. Peters looked up at the steps, at Mr. Darcy's wake. "Married?"

"Yes," said Elizabeth quietly.

Mrs. Peters looked at Elizabeth, pity written all over her face. "Oh, you poor thing. Why, we had no idea, dear. I curse the loss of that letter." She rushed over to Elizabeth, cupping the woman's face in her hands. "You're chilled to the bone, mum. We must get you warmed up." She looked back at the fire. "Oh, heavens, that dog! Stuff and nonsense, and no supper started either." She threw up her hands. "Come with me, mum, come with me. I'll manage it all somehow. I always do." She sighed and hurried over to the steps. She began to climb. A moment later, she looked over her shoulder. "Well, come on, then."

Elizabeth squared her shoulders and followed the woman.

CHAPTER NINE

Mrs. Peters showed Elizabeth into a large bedroom, bigger than two of the drawing rooms in Longbourn. There was a sitting room outside the bedchamber, and Mrs. Peters set about starting a fire in the fireplace and helping Elizabeth out of her coat, which was soaked. She said she would send someone else up immediately, and then she left.

Elizabeth sank down in front of the fire.

It was freezing in her room. Indeed, the whole of Pemberley seemed to be drafty and dank and cold. She had been here but a quarter hour and she already despised the place.

She struggled with tears that were forming in her throat, trying to tell herself that she must not succumb to crying. She distracted herself by thinking of what she would say in her letter to Jane.

Dearest Jane, she composed inwardly. *My husband is a raging maniac who becomes unhinged at the sight of dogs. He terrifies me. My new home is like a dungeon that never gets warm. Write soon, hope all are well at home.*

No, no, no, she mustn't say anything like that.

What positive things could she say of Pemberley?

It is very big. And grand. And... big.

She sighed. Perhaps she could be spared writing a letter tonight. She was tired after all. It had been quite a long journey. She would write tomorrow morning. Surely, in the morning light, things would seem better.

A rapping at her door.

She sprang up from her seat. "Yes?"

The door opened and in came a young lady followed by several other male servants who had brought in her trunk and a large tub.

The girl curtsied. "Mrs. Darcy, my name is Meg, and I shall be your maid. Mrs. Peters thought you would like a bath. They'll be bringing up the water next."

"Oh, that sounds heavenly," said Elizabeth. She smiled at Meg. "It is good to meet you, Meg."

"I hear that Mr. Darcy threw one of his fits," said Meg. "I'm sorry you had to see that. I don't know what your courtship was like, though. Perhaps you've seen him lose his temper already."

"No," said Elizabeth. "Never."

"He never used to be that way," said Meg in a low voice. "Before losing dear Georgiana—that's the late Miss Darcy, his sister, you understand—he was quite happy and amiable. I can't say I ever heard him raise his voice with a servant. We used to boast to anyone who visited about what a wonderful master we had."

"It is the pain of his injuries, I suppose," said Elizabeth.

"It is that dog," said Meg. "He was very clear he didn't want it about, but some of the staff are rather attached to her."

"I don't understand," said Elizabeth. "I gather the dog belonged to someone name Georgie. Is that a nickname for his sister?"

"No, no," said Meg. "That's what they called Mr. Wickham. He grew up in the house as Mr. Darcy's playmate. They ran all over together, being little boys. I daresay Mrs. Peters thought of them both as like her own. She hates it what became of them."

Elizabeth went very still, thinking of what Mrs. Hurst had accused at that dinner all that time ago, that Mr. Darcy had murdered someone named Wickham. "What did become of them?" she whispered.

"Oh, they quarreled after they grew," said Meg. "None are sure why, but Mr. Wickham he stalked out of the house, angry, yelling that Mr. Darcy would see him ruined. And then ... it wasn't long later that the accident happened. However Mr. Wickham was involved, only Mr. Darcy knows."

Elizabeth was quiet, feeling fresh horror wash through her. So, Mr. Darcy had a reason to kill Mr. Wickham, then, or at least, there was enmity between them. And the way that Mr. Darcy felt about that dog, well, she had never seen such hatred. She felt ill.

But then the door opened and the servants were coming in with steaming water to fill the tub, and soon she had no other thoughts than of how wondrous hot water felt on cold skin.

* * *

Dinner was late on account of the servants not having any idea of the arrival of Mr. Darcy. The food, when served, was hot and delicious, and there was a lot of it.

The dining room was enormous. It also boasted a massive fireplace, with orange flames roaring inside it. And yet, the room was still cold, its high ceilings swallowing all the warmth. The walls were stone and so was the floor. The dining table was long and rectangular and the chairs had lion's heads carved into the arms.

Mr. Darcy did not apologize to her for his outburst earlier. He drained several glasses of wine as they ate. When he did speak to her, his voice was a bit slurred.

"You must make yourself at home, Mrs. Darcy," he said. "Explore wherever you would like, except the the east wing. Don't go in there."

"Why not?" she said.

He gave her a tight smile. "Because I forbid it."

She narrowed her eyes at him.

He chuckled, low in his throat. "Mrs. Darcy, I'm aware you're a woman who doesn't take well to being given orders, but I promise you, if you disobey me in this matter, you will live to regret it."

She made herself small, growing interested in her food. Mr. Darcy had been rather awful back in Hertfordshire, but she thought he was worse here. She tried to summon the pity she could usually find for the man, but it had dried up.

Maybe that was for the best. Maybe a man like him used pity to excuse his poor behavior, and he should not be allowed to do so.

She raised her chin, looking down her nose at him. "Do not threaten me again, Mr. Darcy. Somewhere in there, I believe there is a gentleman. I suggest you find him. When next we meet, I would prefer not to converse with whatever barbarian currently is wearing my husband's clothes."

He flinched, looking down at his plate. "Forgive me," he said. "I am... it has been a rather long day."

"For me as well," she said. "Perhaps it might be easier if we finished our meal in silence."

He nodded once.

And they did not speak again that night.

When she went to bed, she had a sudden panic that perhaps Mr. Darcy might come to see her, intent on exercising his husbandly rights to mount her in whatever way men mounted women.

But he did not come, which was good, because she was fearfully tired.

She slipped easily into slumber and slept like the dead all night.

CHAPTER TEN

When she awoke, it was still dark in her room, but she could see that it was only because the draperies were so heavily blocking out the windows. She could see daylight peering around the edges, and so she sprang up to pull aside the curtains.

The sun shone brightly in the sky, but it only illuminated a dreary and dead world below. The grass was brown, the trees were bare, and everything looked a bit soggy from the rain the night before.

Still, sun was better than gloomy rain, so she sat down to compose a letter to Jane, just as she had promised herself. She glossed over the uncomfortable travel and the temperament of her husband. Instead, she wrote of the grandness of her new home and the kindness of the servants she had met. She even wrote of the dogs, but made it seem as if they were also her new friends.

She didn't like it. The letter had an air of forced cheerfulness that Elizabeth knew her sister would see through.

But to put pen to paper and explain how she truly felt would only make it worse. No, it was better to put a bright face on it.

She rang for Meg and dressed. Meg showed her downstairs to the dining room again for breakfast.

The room was brighter now, for there were windows at the top of the room, letting in the morning light. However, the windows only seemed to illuminate cobwebs and dust that had gathered in all the corners. Elizabeth gazed up at them, wondering how a servant would even get up there to clean. They must have to bring in ladders. How often would they even go to the trouble?

"Mrs. Darcy, good morning," came a voice.

She turned and there was Mr. Darcy, striding into the room without his cane, looking almost cheerful.

She smiled. "Good morning."

He went straight to the sideboard, where breakfast was set out and began to serve himself some sausages and ham. "How are you? I am sorry about yesterday. The wet weather seems to make everything hurt so badly. Drinking on top of that did not improve my temperament, I'm afraid. I fear I was quite horrid. My apologies."

Elizabeth did not speak, because she was beginning to be aware that Mr. Darcy had a bit of a pattern. He behaved poorly, and then he apologized about it. But he continued to behave badly. But there was no reason to ruin breakfast, so she inclined her head and said, "Of course, sir."

He regarded her. "That is not forgiveness, but perhaps I don't deserve that." He gestured. "Do you enjoy drinking chocolate? I confess I am more in favor of tea, but I am told that our kitchen staff makes a fine cup."

She came forward. "I do drink chocolate, indeed." She poured herself a cup and tasted it. It was quite good. Sometimes the chocolate at Longbourn was more egg white and spices than actual chocolate. The staff there was wont to make a bar last as long as possible by putting increasingly less chocolate shavings into every pot.

She also filled her plate at the sideboard and sat with Mr. Darcy.

"After breakfast, what would you choose to do?" he said. "I could show you the library or you could play the piano if you liked. You do play, don't you? I am certain I saw you play on one occasion or the other."

"I play, but badly," she said, shaking her head.

He scoffed. " Ah, what does that mean? Women are always trying to measure themselves against some arbitrary standard. It hardly matters. In my experience, all young women are called accomplished, regardless of their actual abilities."

Elizabeth cleared her throat, trying to puzzle that out. Was he agreeing with her that she was bad at the piano? If so, she supposed she didn't care. She *was* awful. Not perhaps so awful as her sister Mary — well, that wasn't fair. Mary was quite diligent about her piano playing, but she'd been cursed with a braying singing voice, and — while she was capable of hitting the proper notes — she was not pleasing to listen to.

Thinking this, she was suddenly hit with a bracing wind of homesickness. It nearly knocked her off her chair. She choked on her chocolate.

Why, she had barely been gone a few days, and she and Mary hardly had a deep and abiding connection, but somehow, she felt the distance between herself and everything she had ever known quite acutely.

Mr. Darcy was still talking. " ... I think that it puts too much pressure on young ladies, and for what reason? To attract someone to marry them? It's preposterous. Women should be allowed to do whatever it is that gives them pleasure, regardless of what society thinks. I think people will become more accomplished at trying their hands at their actual passions, regardless of gender, at any rate. Why, when I was in school, I had no head for dates and history. Simply couldn't keep it in my head. I have somehow survived without being able to name the kings of England in order from William the Conquerer." He paused, looking at her. "I'm sorry, are you well? Here I am, going on and you are quite pale. Is it something you've eaten? Perhaps it doesn't agree with you. I shall ring for something else, just name it."

"No, no, don't go to the trouble." She forced herself to

smile. "I am sorry. I was thinking of something, that is all."

"Something that bothered your constitution?"

She looked down at her plate. "Never mind it. I do find that I agree with what you are saying to some degree. There is a frightful amount of pressure on women to conform to some sort of standard. And I have never, well, quite conformed."

He pointed at her with his fork. "No, I see this about you. I like this about you. It was what I meant when I said that you were not like other women. But I did not mean… of course, you are very feminine and lovely and the epitome of womanhood in a great many ways." He blinked. "I don't seem to be very skilled at giving compliments, do I?"

She chuckled. "I would not say that, sir."

"But you are being kind," he said, cutting his sausage with a fork. "Heaven knows I don't know why. I do not deserve your kindness."

She was not sure how to respond to that. Ought she broach the subject of how he might simply stop doing awful things and then would have no need of constant apologies?

But he spoke again. "I suppose that your lack of interest in the piano means that we ought to find the library instead?"

She laughed. "Yes, I think so."

"Excellent." He speared a bit of sausage and popped it into his mouth.

* * *

The library was as massive as the rest of the place. It was lined with books, and some of the shelves were up so high that a ladder had to be used to reach them. The floor of the library was swathed in carpets and there were high-backed chairs arranged in front of the fireplace, four of them.

"When I was a boy," said Mr. Darcy, gesturing to the chairs, "we would all sit here by the fire, I in one of those chairs which was frightfully too big for me, and my father would read aloud to us. Sometimes Greek myths or epic poetry, but once he did read *Gulliver's Travels*. Also I must say I found all the business about the government at the time went right over my head."

"I think Jonathan Swift was a rather vulgar man," said Elizabeth.

"Well, yes, some of the humor is a bit... base and —"

"Disgusting," said Elizabeth. "He seems obsessed with things better left in chamber pots."

Darcy threw back his head and let out a deep, belly laugh. "Oh, you do have a way of putting things, I must say."

Elizabeth smiled too. "That is not the only thing that stood out to me from the book, of course."

"Yes," said Darcy. "I think it there is much there to elevate it above some its worser tendencies." He turned back to the chair. "But I would say that I am perhaps biased towards it because my father read it to me. I associate it with him."

Elizabeth's heart went out to him. Here she was, with all of her family living, both her parents, all her siblings, and Mr. Darcy had lost everyone and been badly scarred and injured in such a way that caused him constant pain. Perhaps no one could bear that and continue to be polite all the time. Perhaps...

He coughed. "Oh, no, please don't look at me in that way." He turned away from her and went over to one of the chairs, which she now realized was just a bit different than the others. It had obviously been made to copy the style of the other chairs, but it was newer and the color was just slightly different.

If these chairs had been made for the family, then the fourth chair must have been made later, for Mr. Darcy's sister, the one who had died.

He brushed his fingers over the top of it.

Elizabeth had the urge to go to him and embrace him.

Which was ridiculous, of course. Why, you didn't go

about embracing people, not unless they were very small children. It simply wasn't proper. True, he was her husband and they were alone, but...

He looked up at her, his eyes shining. "Well, this is the library. You must come here whenever you like, take as many books as you can carry, and read them wherever takes your fancy. This spot here is quite comfortable, I must say." He smiled.

"Thank you," she said, smiling back.

"Indeed, you must go anywhere you like in the house. It is yours now, too. We are married, and all that is mine is yours. Go and look at it all.

"Except the east wing," she found herself saying, and then she cringed, because he was in a good mood, and why did she have to go and upset him?

But he only bowed his head and was quiet for what seemed like several eternities. Eventually, he raised his gaze to hers. There were tears in his eyes. His voice wasn't strong. "I beg of you, Mrs. Darcy..." He swallowed, composing himself. When he spoke again, his voice was steadier. "Please leave that place alone. Anywhere else, you may go, but that place, *please*..."

* * *

Of course, she went there at once.

She tried to talk herself out of it, but she didn't have the spirit for it. She was more curious about that wing now than ever. The fact it could make Mr. Darcy rage and then nearly cry in front of her, when gentlemen did not cry, *ever*, but especially not in front of their wives, well...

She had to see.

So, that afternoon, while Mr. Darcy was busy in his study going over the books for the estate and all the servants were scurrying around in other areas of the house, she crept up the steps to the east wing.

As she did, the air grew colder. They did not light fires in this part of the house. No one came here. She looked over her shoulder, making sure no one was following her, and then she kept going.

The east wing was dark, though there was light coming through a window at the end of the hallway. All of the doors here were shut, and she could see clouds of air coming from her mouth when she breathed. It was quite cold.

She pushed open the first door, and stepped into a vast nursery. It was still full of all manner of toys, two rocking horses and stacks of blocks and balls. Rows of dolls were arranged on a shelf in between the windows. There was a bed frame, and a mattress on it, but the bed was covered in a number of dolls as well, soft cloth ones with yarn hair, who were arranged there. It didn't look as if the bed was often slept in.

At the far end of the room, the nursery gave way to what looked like a classroom. There was a desk, an easel for painting, and a piano.

Elizabeth stood there at the juncture between the two rooms, and imagined that this was where Mr. Darcy's sister Georgiana must have spent most of her days. She did not know much about Georgiana, only that she was quite a lot younger than Mr. Darcy, and perhaps he had striven to keep her young, not having her leave the nursery, even as she grew older.

Elizabeth left the nursery, closing the door behind herself and then she opened the next door.

It was a bedroom, much like her own bedroom, in fact, although it was a good deal smaller. Elizabeth stopped to look at the desk, which still had a stack of paper sitting on it. She picked one up off the top, expecting to find a letter, but instead it was a sonnet of sorts, written in a girlish hand. The title was, "A Verse on my Governess Miss Younge."

At the bottom, Elizabeth could see that it had been signed by Miss Georgiana Darcy.

She set the sonnet back on the desk and left that room as well.

The next bedroom was larger, and there were a great many clothes in the wardrobe, all the perfect size for a young girl. This must have been Georgiana ' s room. Elizabeth walked around, afraid to touch anything. The place was exactly as Georgiana had left it. It hadn't been touched.

There were papers on Georgiana's desk too, but these looked as though they had been crumpled up and then later smoothed out.

There were three different attempts at the same subject, which was to beg permission of her older brother to spend more time on horseback and less time practicing the piano and learning French.

Everyone says I am already very good at the piano, and why must I get even better? I know I will find someone to marry even if I am dreadful at it, because I am an heiress.

Elizabeth chuckled to herself. Yes, she could see why that attempt had been abandoned. It was the sort of thing a girl might say, but she recognized it was not polite to flaunt her status, even to her own brother.

Then Elizabeth thought of the conversation at breakfast with a pang.

Of course Mr. Darcy would now think that women should do what they liked. How guilty he must feel for depriving Georgiana of pleasure in her short life.

But he couldn't have known she would be killed. No one could predict such accidents. Death came for everyone, though when it came for the young, it was monstrous.

She sighed. It had been wrong of her to come into this place. It was a shrine of sorts, to a girl that Elizabeth had never known, and she was disrupting it all with her presence.

She hurried out of the room, feeling a bit ashamed of herself.

She shut the door, or she tried, but it seemed it was catching on something, and so she opened it again, and then tried to pull it closed.

This time it latched.

When she looked up from the closed door, she realized she wasn't alone.

Mr. Darcy was standing in the middle of the hallway, not four feet from her.

CHAPTER ELEVEN

Elizabeth's jaw worked.

Caught. Of course I would be caught. It's as if I've never read a novel in my life. I know what happens to curious young women. It's Pandora's box all over again. Eve in the garden. I know better.

Mr. Darcy stalked over to her and took her by the arm.

She didn't offer him any resistance.

Stiffly, he dragged her out of the wing, and they did not stop walking until they were far enough away that the house had a semblance of warmth to it.

Then he let go of her. "I hope you're pleased with yourself," he said in a flat voice.

"I-I'm most incredibly sorry, sir," she said. "I should have respected your wishes. I shouldn't have intruded upon your sister's memory. I... it was unforgivable of me."

He didn't say anything.

"Truly, I did not know what to expect when I went up there," she said. "You might have simply told me it was your sister's old quarters and that you didn't want them disturbed, and I would have understood. I would not have gone there."

"I do not like to speak of her," said Darcy, and there was a hint of steel in the undercurrent of his tone now.

"Of course," said Elizabeth. "Of course. Well, I am sorry. I will never go back." She bowed her head. "Truly, my sincere apologies." Then she turned and started away from him. She would go back to her room, and perhaps read a book and —

He took her by the arm again, stopping her movement. "*Are* you pleased with yourself?"

She looked at him. They were so close now. His face was mere inches from hers, and they hadn't been this close since the time he kissed her.

Warmth went through her, followed by icy cold.

"Well?" he said.

"Of course not."

"Defying me doesn't give you some kind of pleasure?" His voice had dropped in register again.

"No," she breathed.

He moved closer, and his gaze flicked down to her lips and then back up to her eyes. "I ordered you not to go, and I recognize that was barbarous of me, so I asked you, with as much civility as I could muster. And yet, still, you ignored my wishes."

"I don't know what else to say. I am sorry. Truly sorry."

"I would have a care, madam," he whispered. "It would not be wise for you to make me angry." He let go of her and stepped back.

She nearly lost her balance, but she managed to right herself.

And then she hurried away from him as quickly as she possibly could.

* * *

Meg asked Elizabeth what had happened, but Elizabeth did not want to speak of it. She was ashamed of herself, truly, and she spent the rest of the afternoon staring senselessly at the pages of books. She found she could not concentrate, that she would get to the end of a page and find she had only pronounced all the words in her head but had not attended to them, so she did not actually know what they meant.

She would start again, going to the top of the page, but only comprehend half of it.

When it was time for dinner, she was happy of the

distraction, even though it meant she would have to face Mr. Darcy again.

She did feel badly for what she had done, but, she reasoned, what was it against all the things that Mr. Darcy had done to her? It didn't even compare. She had apologized, but it was the only she needed to apologize for.

He must forgive her, and in return, she would forgive him for forcing the marriage.

Then they could begin again, on even ground.

It was a reasonable proposition, more than fair, really, because what she had done did not even compare to how Mr. Darcy had wronged her. He must agree to it.

But when she entered the dining room, Mr. Darcy was not there.

She was informed he had decided to take his dinner in his room that night. She would be eating alone.

This perturbed her more than she might have expected it would. She had spent the entire afternoon alone, thinking about speaking to him, and he had hidden from her.

Was this the way things were going to be for the whole of her marriage to this man? Was it going to be a series of explosions, followed by Mr. Darcy avoiding doing anything to correct the situation?

Because that, she decided, was the true problem for Mr. Darcy. He was stuck in a pattern of behavior, stuck in his ways, stuck in the past.

She didn't finish her meal. She threw her napkin on the table and got up from the table. The footman asked her, concerned, if everything was to her liking, and she responded that it was delicious and she would like it sent up to her room as well, that they could extinguish the fire in the dining room and dispense with all the pageantry.

But then she did not go to her room but went through the house, seeking out Mr. Darcy.

She found him in a room upstairs, curled around a glass of whisky, staring into the fire. "Listen, Mr. Darcy, we had best settle all this."

He looked up at her, and she could see from the way his movements were exaggerated that he was drunk. "Why, it's my lovely wife."

This angered her. "Are you a drunkard as well, sir? Shall we add that to your many sins? Pray, what is it that you have about you to recommend you to anyone?"

He laughed. " Well, you are in a fine temper, are you not?"

"Why did you not join me at dinner?"

"I did not think I'd be good company."

"Indeed, you are rarely good company," she said.

" Well, that may be true, " he said. " Which is why I removed myself from you."

" But I wished to speak to you, " she said. "I wished to make some sort of peace between us, but you did not appear, and now… well, now I find that I want badly to wring your neck."

"Truly?" he said, arching an eyebrow. "I did not realize you were craving my company so deeply. Perhaps I am growing on you."

" It is not because you did not come down for dinner. Well, it is not only that. That is one part of a great many things that seems to raise my ire."

" Yes, I suppose you mean to enumerate them? That is why you've come here to interrupt my peace and quiet? " His eyes flashed.

"Oh, are you becoming angry? I'm not to anger you, am I? You say that would not be wise, but I am not interested in any more of your threats. " She folded her arms over her chest. "What do you expect from your future? Will this be the way it is until the end of your days? Morosely going through your sister's rooms, allowing her things to gather dust, leaving her old toys there like some kind of shrine?"

His nostrils flared. "I have told you that I do not like to speak of her."

"That is the nursery of the house." She pointed in the direction of the east wing. "Where did you expect our own children would play and sleep?"

"Our children?" He let out a wild laugh. "You cannot be serious."

"Why not? You must move out of this cloud of sadness in the past. You have been dogged with tragedy, sir, but your entire life need not be about pain and sadness. We could have guests for dinners, fill that enormous dining room. We could host balls. We could have a marriage, a life, together, but if you will not let go—"

"Stop," he snapped, and he got to his feet.

"I won't stop," she said. "Perhaps I'm saying this wrong. I don't know. If I could have not raised my voice and been gentle, perhaps... but I am saying it anyway, and I am trying to say that we must wipe it all clean, our trespasses to each other, and start anew. This marriage, you said you wanted me, and I am here, and yet you..."

"What?" He advanced on her. "What is it you want? Do you know how children are made, madam?"

She nodded. "Of course."

"Explain it to me."

She blushed, looking down at her feet. "I hardly think this change of subject is warranted, sir."

"So, you don't know."

"There is... the man m-mounts the woman and there is... I have seen animals coupling, sir. I am no blushing innocent." She raised her chin.

His lips parted, and something came over his expression something almost harsh, but something eager as well. "And you are willing to do that with this?" He pointed at his face.

She licked her lips. She searched for her voice, but it had deserted her. She stepped closer to him and she reached out one tentative finger to trace the rope of angry red flesh that marred his face.

He shut his eyes, going stock still.

She let out an audible breath, a hissing sigh.

He seized her about the waist. He kissed her.

The kiss was like before, like on the dance floor, his tongue in her mouth, teasing wild pleasures through her, making her body alight with tingles. The kiss was warmth and sweetness and everything good, and she was undone.

It went on for some time, and when he stopped, he trailed smaller kisses over the corner of her mouth, down to her jaw and onto her neck.

She gasped.

He pulled away to look at her.

And she took a step backward, shaking from head to toe. Without a word, she turned and ran from the room.

* * *

Elizabeth shut the door to her room and tried to still the wild pounding of her pulse, which was going at a terrifying pace, and she could feel it at her wrists and at her neck, and she shut her eyes and then opened them and then shut them again.

All at once, she drew herself up, blinking. She threw herself at her desk, clawing about for some paper and a pen and ink.

She smoothed out a fresh sheet and began to write.

Dear Jane, I have been lying to you all along about my husband. He wants to be intimate but I cannot allow it, and I have run from him, just now, because he is a beast. A dreadful beast, yes. And he is ugly. I have never seen such an ugly man, and I will not, I can not allow him to touch me.

A choking sob escaped her lips and she picked up the piece of paper and crumpled it into a ball.

She got out a new sheet of paper.

Dear Jane, she wrote. *My husband is the most cruel and capricious man I have ever met. He is likely to be in a foul temper whenever I meet him. I cannot know from one moment to the next which man I will meet. He can be good and kind and even generous, but more often than not he is selfish and angry and sarcastic. And when he kissed me, I had to run from him because I cannot kiss a man like that. I cannot even be married to him. I don' t know what I've done to myself and I –*

At once, she picked up the sheet of paper and ripped it in two. Ink smudged on her fingertips. She rubbed it into her skin, irritated.

She sat back in her chair, and she gazed at the ceiling.

Then she sat forward again and her movements were slower, more deliberate.

She selected another sheet of paper.

Dear Jane, what was it like when you knew you were in love with Mr. Bingley? Did it feel rather lovely, as though you had been surrounded by softness and light? It must have, because Mr. Bingley is so amiable and good and cheerful. If I could have it another way, I would fall in love with a man such as him. I would not fall in love with a man such as Mr. Darcy, even if he summons within me feelings that I cannot control, that seem to consume every part of my body, that seem to fray me at the edges and then set the frayed edges on fire. I would not have it, but I am afraid it is happening. Will I survive loving a man such as this? Have I lost my wits? Jane, I am frightened.

She left the letter there, unfinished, and she got up and went to the window of her bedroom. She pulled aside the curtains and peered up at the night sky, which was dotted with a sea of stars. Tremors went through her, and her shoulders shook, but her eyes stayed dry.

After a time, it passed, and she was tired. She would not send Jane that letter, of course, but she did not throw it away. She folded it up and put it in a drawer. Then she rang for Meg to help her undress.

She fell into bed soon enough, exhausted.

CHAPTER TWELVE

She ran from his kiss.

Of course she ran.

Why had he done it?

Darcy wondered if he would ever learn to check himself. He had done nothing except transgress against this woman, and he continued to do so, much to his horror.

Sometimes, he did not know himself. He had the feeling that somehow he had been inhabited by another man when he had been injured, and he was not sure if he liked this new man that resided within his skin. He was certain that Georgiana would not have liked him.

But then his sister had often been angry with him. He had been too strict with her. She had been kept away from society, and she had been bursting at the seams for more, for adventure, for fun. Why couldn't he have indulged her a bit more?

Perhaps then, Wickham would not have been able to entice her.

But there was no worrying about it now, was there?

He could not change anything.

He told himself not to go after his wife, to leave her be. If she wanted his company, she could seek him out again, and he was certain she did not want his company.

But as the night wore on, and he had more and more glasses of strong drink, his better judgment was eroded.

He found himself outside her door, a candle in hand.

He tried the door and he stepped inside. It was dark in

there, and she was asleep. He came too close to her, shining the candle over her face so that he could look upon her, even though he knew he risked waking her. When she woke and found him here, watching her sleep, she would not be pleased.

She was so beautiful, lying there with her hair splayed out on the pillow, her eyes closed, that his chest hurt.

He didn't deserve this beautiful woman for a wife. He had gotten her by trickery and by base behavior. Now, she was his, and he was the very devil to her.

Still, he gazed at her, and he could not tear his gaze away.

"Listen," he said in a low whisper. "Elizabeth." He liked the way the name felt coming out of his lips. He sighed, and then he murmured it again. "Elizabeth."

She stirred in her sleep.

He jerked back.

But she did not wake, so he continued. " Elizabeth, I promise to you, I will never touch you again. Not unless you specifically request me to touch you."

She stirred again.

He chuckled softly. "Let's be honest, you'll never do that. Why should you? I don't blame you for it. I am sorry to have been such a bad man so far, but I want to be better, whatever that means, and I will start by respecting your wishes. I promise. I will take nothing else from you that you have not freely given."

* * *

The next morning, Elizabeth broke her fast alone. She was rather relieved when Mr. Darcy did not appear. She did not seek him out, even when he was not there for luncheon or dinner. Admittedly, his presence at luncheon was not something to be counted upon, anyway. She was used to not seeing him then, and sometimes she was not hungry and asked only to have a bit of bread and butter and tea.

A week passed, and she did not see him at all. She did

not report this in her daily letters to Jane, however, thinking it might sound odd. Nor did she write that she had fallen in love with a beastly man who was cruel and selfish. She wrote mostly of the house, of the servants, of the gardens which she walked in when it was not too cold.

And Jane's letters had started to arrive, telling her of all the news at home. Jane told her that Lydia was now a very special friend of Mrs. Forster, Colonel Forster's wife, and that Lydia spent much of her time dreaming of being a wife to an officer in the regiment, and that her mother encouraged it, while her father muttered about silly girls.

She wrote that their father missed her very much, and that he asked to have Elizabeth's letters after Jane had read them aloud to the family to read them himself. She wrote that Mary was learning a new piece on the piano, and that she played it day and night, much to the chagrin of everyone in the family, who were all quite tired of hearing it.

Most excitingly, she wrote that she was engaged, that Mr. Bingley had come to ask for her hand, and that she was incandescently happy, which made Elizabeth feel happy too. After the announcement, the Hursts had quit Netherfield, taking Miss Bingley along with them. Jane expressed her regret at no longer having the joy of their society, and Elizabeth snorted aloud, thinking that her sister was far too kindly sometimes.

When Mr. Darcy did appear at mealtimes again, so much time had passed that they did not speak of the events that occurred that night, when she ran away. He was always polite and solicitous to her, and to the servants as well, at least whenever she observed him.

They spoke of only trivialities. The weather. The food. The servants.

There was a bit of interest amongst one of the footmen and one of the kitchen maids, who were in some kind of a flirtation, and who everyone was speculating about, especially Meg, who spoke of it whenever she saw Elizabeth.

Apparently, Mr. Darcy's valet talked to him of it too.

So, she and Mr. Darcy gossiped about the servants and whether or not they would be married, and it was all frightfully domestic and nothing about her life was amiss at all.

Sometimes, of course, she thought about the future, and it made her feel like she might lose her mind and run raving into the night, so she endeavored not to think of it after all.

Because she knew that she could not go on in this way forever. This was no way to live, this half-marriage with a man who she did not know and who refused to speak with her about anything real.

She almost preferred it when he had been raging and awful. At least that had been something. Now...

Well, she would tell herself that even if she couldn't bear it forever, she could bear it for the next day, or even the next fortnight, and she would resolve to make it through that time only.

The future was something distant, something she did not ponder.

* * *

Darcy kept his word to himself. He did not touch his wife. He did not do anything remotely offensive when she was observing him.

But he could not stop himself from going at night to watch her sleep, even though he knew this was wronging her in its way. Watching her when she was not aware of it, when she had not given permission, it was taking something from her, even if that thing was intangible.

He knew he should go, because when he did, when he gazed at her sleeping and beautiful, he wanted her so badly it made him think he might go witless and raving.

He thought of touching her. He thought of having her. She was his wife, and he was well within his rights to demand to share her bed and to be with her.

He wouldn't, of course. He had made his vow.

But he imagined it, gazing down at her in the candlelight. He hated himself for it.

Every night, he vowed he would not go to her. He did various things to try to prevent it, going so far as to move his wardrobe in front of the door to his bedroom.

But nothing prevented it, because no matter what he moved into his way, he could always simply move it out of the way again, and then he made his way through the halls to her room and stayed there with her, indulging in his wretched fantasies.

One night, she stirred. She turned over, blinking against the light of the candle.

He swore, blowing out the candle.

She let out a little cry, and it was now too dark for him to see, but it sounded as though she sat up in bed, drawing the covers up around her. "Who's there?" she cried out, her voice thin and frightened.

He didn't answer.

"Who is that?" she said.

He blinked and blinked until his eyes adjusted and he moved soundlessly over the carpets and out of her room, never answering her.

* * *

"You were in my room last night," said Elizabeth at the breakfast table the following morning.

Mr. Darcy looked into his tea, his expression unreadable.

"Don't deny it," she said.

"I suppose that would be folly," he said, but he said it into his tea, without meeting her gaze.

Elizabeth drew herself up. She had determined to speak to him about this, because it had been difficult for her to get back to sleep after waking in the manner she had been roused. At first, half-asleep, she had been plagued by fanciful fears—a horrible monster prowling the hallways of Pemberley, or perhaps climbing in and out of windows.

But as she had wakened completely, she realized this

was not likely, and that it must have been Mr. Darcy himself. She had lain awake, then, pondering what he might have been doing there, and she could not make sense of it. She resolved to talk to him about it.

"I am quite sorry, madam," said Mr. Darcy. "There are no excuses for encroaching upon you in such a way. I knew that it was wrong when I did it, but I did not seem to be able to stop myself, even so. I wish that I were not a man drawn so deeply to dark and sinful actions."

This confused her further. "Why do you say this? What were you doing there?"

He retreated into his chair, bowing his shoulders around his tea cup. "Well, nothing."

"Nothing? And yet you apologize so fiercely. I suppose this is like what you said about Othello, that time we met in the stairs at Netherfield."

"Ah, but Othello had the very devil whispering in his ear. I have no Iago to blame."

"You said that Othello was too easily led to murder," said Elizabeth. A chill went through her. "Were you there to harm me?"

He straightened, tea sloshing out onto the floor. " Of course not!"

"Well, then what was it all about, sir?"

"I was... looking at you."

She raised her eyebrows.

He set the nearly empty tea cup back in its saucer with a clatter.

"Why?" she said.

"You are... pleasant to look upon," he muttered.

She was confused, too confused to know what to say.

He got up out of his chair, seizing at his cane and striding away from her, toward the massive fireplace in the dining room.

She stood up too. "I don't understand."

"Why not?" His voice was sharp. "You know that I want

you. I have made that plain."

Her body suddenly tightened. She gripped the back of the chair for balance.

It was quiet.

She opened her mouth to speak, but he was so far away now, and she did not wish to shout at him across the room when they were speaking of such things. So, she let go of the back of the chair and went after him.

He stood in front of the fire, leaning on his cane. The flames reflected against the scar on his face, making it look more grotesque.

She stopped next to him, clasping her hands together. "If you were visiting me to claim your husbandly rights —"

"No."

"You are, of course, entitled —"

"No." He glanced at her. "Let us leave this subject, madam. I swear to you, I will not come to your room at night again."

She swallowed. "Mr. Darcy, we have not spoken of... what happened all those nights ago, when we..." She found it hard to say the word.

He turned his dark gaze on her.

"Kissed," she finally managed, her voice barely audible.

His eyes held her own for several long moments.

"I'm sorry that I ran from you," she said. "I should not have, truly. And I did not think..." She furrowed her brow. "For the life of me, I can't understand why I did not think of how you must have interpreted my actions, but now I see that I must have made you think that I regretted —"

A series of loud barks.

They both looked up to see the dog, Lady, the one that had been lounging in front of the fire the first night they'd arrived, running across the room toward them.

Mr. Darcy's fingers tightened around his cane.

CHAPTER THIRTEEN

Elizabeth reached out and put her hand on his arm, but why she did it, she wasn't sure. Could she calm him with a touch? Could she stop the anger that she could see had already overtaken his body?

He was stiff and his face was twisted, his nostrils flared. He flung aside his cane and went after the dog, moving with surprising speed and agility.

"Mr. Darcy!" called Elizabeth.

" Oh, heavens! " said Mrs. Peters, appearing in the doorway where the dog had come from. "Sir!"

Mr. Darcy tackled Lady, arms around her neck. The two went down onto the floor, struggling. The dog was whining and growling, snapping its teeth, and Mr. Darcy was squeezing it as if he meant it harm.

Elizabeth rushed forward and so did Mrs. Peters.

"She's only a dog!" cried Mrs. Peters.

Elizabeth fell to her knees and wrapped her arms around her husband's chest. "Stop it!"

Darcy did stop, seemingly shocked by Elizabeth's touch. He looked at her over his shoulder.

She let go of him, and she stood up, thinking about how she had not realized how firm and solid and muscular his back would be. She knew he was wounded, but he was still quite strong. She felt flustered.

Mrs. Peters had the dog. "Please, sir."

Mr. Darcy scrambled to his feet, tossing at his hair, which had fallen into his eyes. "Please? You beg for the dog?

I thought you found another home for her."

Mrs. Peters shook her head. "We've been keeping her in the kitchens, I'm afraid. She's a good dog, and the others are her littermates, and we all love her so, and..."

"Mrs. Peters, who is the master of this house?" Mr. Darcy's eyes flashed.

"Well, you are, sir," said Mrs. Peters. "But—"

"Then, when I give an order, are you not to obey it?"

"Yes, sir." Mrs. Peters hung her head.

"Have the dog gone by the end of the day," said Mr. Darcy imperiously, "or you shall go with it."

"Mr. Darcy!" exclaimed Elizabeth.

Darcy turned to look at her. "Oh, you don't approve?"

"How long has Mrs. Peters been your housekeeper?" said Elizabeth. "Why, did she not know you when you were a boy? Has she not given a lifetime of service to your family? And you think to dismiss her?"

"I shall ask you the same question, *dear* wife," said Mr. Darcy, his voice like ice. "Who is the master of this house?'

"Well, I won't answer it, because you're behaving in such a manner as to be positively horrid."

"It's a simple request, really," said Mr. Darcy, going back to the table, this time with a bit of a limp in his gait. "I want the dog gotten rid of. I don't care what you do with it. Slit its throat for all I care."

"Kill the dog?" said Elizabeth, aghast.

"Perhaps I should do it myself," said Darcy, who had arrived at the table. He bent over it, bracing his hands on the edge, his head bent down. "It seems that's the only way my wishes are carried out in this house."

Mrs. Peters cleared her throat. "It is truly not Lady's fault. Why, Georgie didn't even care for her, and you are punishing her for—"

Mr. Darcy swept the plates and cups and silverware off the table and they all shattered against the floor.

Mrs. Peter's voice died in her throat.

Elizabeth flinched.

Mr. Darcy turned, and he was trembling with rage. "Pray, don't mention his name ever again in my presence. If I don't wish to see the dog, I don't wish to hear you call him *Georgie*, in the name of *God*, Mrs. Peters. It's as if no one *believes* me when I tell you what that man was."

Mrs. Peters shook her head, her mouth working as she searched for words. "No, of course not. I'm sorry. I will... Lady will..."

Darcy started for her.

Mrs. Peters backed away, dragging the dog with her. She looked frightened.

Elizabeth went to intercept him. "Perhaps you should take a moment alone, husband, in order to calm yourself."

Darcy rounded on her. "Oh, you think to tell me how to handle my affairs?"

"I think that you are being a monster," said Elizabeth. "And whatever there is in you, sir, there is not only monstrousness, so when you let it out—"

"You are mistaken," said Darcy. "Shut your mouth."

"I shan't," said Elizabeth. "I am your wife, and if no one else is here to check your bad behavior, then—"

"That is something we shall remedy," said Mr. Darcy. With that, he turned, looking around the room. Eventually, he spied his cane. He went to it, swept it off the floor and left the room.

Elizabeth didn't know what to do. She turned to Mrs. Peters. "I'm so dreadfully sorry. I don't know why he's this way."

"It's you I'm sorry for, mum," said Mrs. Peters. "Married to that. He wasn't always this way, you know. He was the sweetest little boy." Her lower lip trembled.

"Yes," said Elizabeth. "Well..." And she thought of the fact that she had fallen in love with Mr. Darcy and wondered if she could fall out of love, if—in fact—she was falling out of love just now, as this was all unfolding.

"I should see to the dog," said Mrs. Peters. "Have someone clean this up." She gestured to the broken dishes.

"Yes," said Elizabeth. "I think I shall retire to my room."

But when she got to her room, the door was open, and Mr. Darcy was inside. He was inside her wardrobe, tearing out her dresses and hurling them onto the floor. "I can't find your trunk," he said when he saw her. "Perhaps you know where the maid has stored it?"

"What are you doing?" said Elizabeth.

"Helping you pack," he said.

"What?"

"Let's be truthful with each other. You don't want to be married to me, and I was a fool for going through with it. I thought to be as honorable as I could in the face of my dishonor, but I shouldn't have done such a thing to you. Now, I'll fix it. I'll send you back to your family."

"You can't send me back. We've been married for two months. There is no undoing that."

"The marriage is not consummated. We'll get it annulled. It'll be as if it never was."

"That's... you can't simply —"

"I'll give you money," said Mr. Darcy, throwing out a creamy morning dress. "Why I didn't think of this before, I don't know, but I have thought of it now, and if I pay you enough, surely it will make up for all the hardship that I have caused you."

"Take your hands off my clothes!"

He laughed at her, a wild laugh, and he sounded insane.

Maybe the sound of it infected her. She waded over her wardrobe to him, and she grabbed his arms to stop him.

They wrestled for a moment, but he was far too strong for her to have any effect on him.

He soon had her by the arm, and he was dragging her over her clothes — which were strewn on the floor — and out of her bedroom.

She struggled. "Let me go. Take your hands off me!"

111

"Indeed, if I give you enough money, you can buy new dresses. Why bother to pack them?" He tugged her down the stairs.

"Please!" she said, trying to get free of him. She was frightened, but underneath all that, she was furious. The fury was growing inside her, climbing into her throat.

They crossed the vast expanse of the main entryway, and Mr. Darcy threw open the front door. "There. Go!"

The cold air swirled over the threshold.

It was snowing.

CHAPTER FOURTEEN

Darcy gazed dumbly into the snow, which was already laying on the ground, turning the blades of brown grass white.

His wife wrenched her arm free. "You wretch!"

He turned to look at her, feeling as if the snow had extinguished something hot and glowing inside him, coals of bright rage. But now, he felt exhausted and spent. He shut the door.

"Never touch me again," said Elizabeth, her voice quiet but serious.

He swallowed.

"I'll leave," she said. "I will. There is nothing that could induce me to remain here with you any longer."

"It's snowing," he said softly. "You can't leave now. It wouldn't be safe."

"You really thought to throw me out, here and now? You thought to simply pack me off and solve the pesky problem of having a wife? Is it that awful to have someone pointing out that you are behaving worse than the devil himself?"

His jaw twitched. "Listen… it wasn't you I was angry with. I shouldn't have taken it out on—"

"It was the dog, then?" said Elizabeth. "Or Mrs. Peters?"

He hung his head.

"I know," said Elizabeth. "Perhaps it was *Georgie*."

He winced. He couldn't look at her.

"Killing him wasn't enough?" she said. "You didn't

extinguish your hatred of the man when you murdered him?"

Now, he looked up at her, confused. "What are you saying?"

"You are..." She wrung out her hands. "I don't know why I thought there was anything good in you at all."

"I suppose I deserve that."

"You can't think that simply giving me money will actually fix what it is you've done to me."

"I don't see why not," he said.

"If you annul our marriage, it's all well and good for you. You'll still be Mr. Darcy of Pemberley. You can get married again. But I shall never be able to do so. I shall be ruined and used up, no matter that you never touched me. No one will—"

"I shall give you so much money that you can have your pick of pretty fortune hunting men," said Darcy, lifting his chin. "You can marry again, if that's what you wish. You can be Lady Something-or-Other. I guarantee there are a great many heirs out there with nothing but worthless titles, and they'd be glad enough for an influx of income."

Her lips parted as he spoke, and she stared at him, utterly flummoxed. "You would... that is... you couldn't be so foolhardy to part with so much of your fortune."

"Couldn't I? Haven't I treated you very badly? Don't you deserve it for what I have done to your reputation and your future? And what is it you suppose I might be saving it for? I shan't marry. I am not a good husband. I shan't have heirs, and I shall simply watch everything crumble around me for the rest of my days. There is no reason to hang on."

"But ..." She bit down on her bottom lip, and she appeared to be torn between saying something to him and staying quiet.

He'd had enough talk for one morning. "Get out of my sight."

"What?"

"Go." He nodded at the steps. "Oversee your maid packing your dresses. As soon as the snow is cleared, you will leave."

* * *

Elizabeth dashed off a letter to Jane, telling her everything that occurred, how Mr. Darcy had raged and broken plates, how he had dragged her down the steps and tried to throw her out of his house, how she was glad to be leaving him.

If she was truly going home, there was no reason to send the letter. She could tell Jane when she arrived.

The horrid truth was that she wasn't sure she wanted to go home.

She instructed Meg to hang all her dresses back in her wardrobe and to mend the ones that had been damaged by Mr. Darcy. Then she sat at her desk and composed another letter to Jane.

I cannot still be in love with him. Surely, I've fallen out of love with him. He is a monster, and he will not change. He will only get worse. It is the height of stupidity to want to stay with such a man. So, what has gone wrong with me, my dear sister, that I am in no hurry to leave him?

I feel as though his anger is not about me or about the dog or anyone in the house. I feel as though it has something to do with that Georgie Wickham, whoever he was. And whatever I said, I don't think Mr. Darcy did kill him. Or if he did, I don't think he meant it. Perhaps it was one of these rages that comes over him. Perhaps he was not in control of himself.

But that's not an excuse.

And it shouldn't reassure me. After all, what if one of those rages came over him, and he and I had a child? I could not bear that. Of course, it is impossible for there to be a child, and I am rather sure he will never touch me, so there is no worry on that score.

I have to try, Jane, don't you understand? We are already married. The damage is done. I have to attempt to see if I can find a good man in him. If he can work through his anger and leave it behind, perhaps things could be different.

True, he has not ever said that he loved me, but he has professed to want me, which is a close thing, is it not?

Why do I feel as though I am the most idiotic woman in all of England and that I should be bodily restrained and carried away from this man for my own safety? What is it about him that affects me so?

She folded up this letter too, putting it in her drawer, never to be sent.

Outside, the snow continued.

She dined alone. Mr. Darcy was nowhere to be found, even when she went looking for him in the house. She did not go to the east wing, though. Perhaps he was there.

When she woke the next morning, the snow had stopped.

* * *

The lack of frozen water falling from the sky seemed to clear her wits. She gazed out the window at the vast expanse of unbroken snow, and she knew that she would leave.

It was ridiculous to stay. Mr. Darcy was quite unpredictable, and he might do all manner of dreadful things to her. She would leave, and if he would really give her all that money, life would be bearable afterward.

She could travel with Jane and Bingley, pay her own way. Why, with that much money, she would be very like a rich widow. She would be free to do as she pleased. She could buy a house in town. Nothing could stand in her way. She wouldn't need to marry again. It would mean she would never have children, though.

That saddened her.

But she resolved that she would have many chances to be an aunt, what with all of her sisters, and she would take full advantage of that.

Yes, she would leave, because it was the intelligent thing to do.

Of course, it was going to break her heart.

That was ridiculous too. How she could love this man, she didn't understand. It made no sense at all. Such are the ways of a wayward heart, she supposed.

A broken heart would not be pleasant, but she could bear it up.

She called for Meg, dressed for breakfast, went down to the dining room.

Mr. Darcy was nowhere to be found again.

Well, perhaps it would be easier not to see him. She broke her fast and then went to a sitting room upstairs, determined to read and look out the window on the snow.

But when she did, she saw that there were four or five men gathered outside in the snow, tramping about in it and ruining the pristine perfection of the surface. They appeared to be trying to move a large branch that had fallen off one of the trees near the drive. Probably it had fallen under the weight of the snow.

She squinted.

Was that Mr. Darcy out there? What was he doing? He couldn't be working with the men in the snow, could he?

But yes, there was his cane.

And then she thought that there was no leaving Pemberley with that large branch in the road. He must be eager to move it.

She closed her book and called for Meg to dress her warmly.

Within a quarter hour, she was outside, strolling through the snow to Mr. Darcy.

He was swinging an ax. She supposed the tree branch was too big to move on its own and that it would be more easily removed in pieces.

She stopped short, watching him. The movement of his body was mesmerizing. He raised the ax and then it bit into the wood, and then he raised it again. She watched, her lips parted, soundless.

"Sir, that is enough," said one of the men nearby. "Let me finish that for you."

"I'm not an invalid, Mr. Marshall," said Mr. Darcy, who

was a little out of breath, but sounded invigorated and happy. Then he caught sight of Elizabeth, and he very nearly dropped the ax. "Madam, what are you doing out here?"

"You're quite eager to be rid of me, I see," she said.

"What?" Mr. Darcy scoffed. He handed the ax over to Mr. Marshall and crossed to her. "Why, even after this is moved out of the way, it'll be some time before the roads are passable again. All this snow? It's not going anywhere and neither are you."

"So, then, what are you doing out here?"

"Well, I was walking with the dogs." Mr. Darcy gestured across the yard, and there were three dogs running in the snow.

"All of the dogs?"

"I have given Lady a pardon," said Mr. Darcy. He looked about. "Where the devil is my cane?" Then he saw it, sticking up out of the snow, and he started for it.

"You have?" She went with him.

He found the cane and leaned on it. "Yes, it has been pointed out to me that visiting punishment on a poor beast for the actions of her previous master is…" He shrugged, giving her a helpless smile. "Madness."

She couldn't help but smile back.

"Lady can stay," said Darcy. "She is a good dog, and the staff is fond of her. I was wrong to be harsh with her."

"You decided this? When?"

"This morning, I suppose." He sucked in air through his nose. "There's something about snow, isn't there?"

"Yes," she said quietly. "There is."

He pointed at the dogs with his cane. "Well, if you are out here, would you like to walk with me and the dogs?"

She hesitated. "I don't see why not."

They took off together through the white powder. It was magical stuff, so beautiful.

Elizabeth looked at him sidelong, feeling more confused than ever. "And, um, what about Lady's previous master?"

He turned to her sharply. "Please, it's so nice out here. Don't ruin it."

She nodded. "All right."

They walked together, and the dogs came running for them, cavorting in the fluffy whiteness, tongues hanging out, balls of fur and joy.

She petted Lady's head, and scratched Rex under his chin.

Mr. Darcy sighed. "I feel as if all I do is apologize to you."

She laughed. "Yes. In between being horrible, that is."

He chuckled. "Well, I'm not going to this time. It's pointless. We can be civil to each other for this last remaining time. You'll be leaving soon enough."

She nodded. "I will."

They held each other's gaze for a minute, and she thought she saw something pained in his expression, and she was horrified her own pain was visible too.

But then there was a shout from the men who were wresting with the branch.

She and Mr. Darcy both turned to look.

Darcy's brow furrowed in concern. "That's Mr. Nelson on his back."

"Oh, no," said Elizabeth. Nelson was one of the footmen, the one everyone gossiped over, who was likely to marry one of the kitchen maids.

Together, they took off towards the men and the branch. Mr. Darcy, despite his cane and his limp, got out ahead of her and reached them first.

When she got there, Darcy was on the ground next to Nelson, whose face was very white.

"What happened?" said Elizabeth.

Darcy looked up at her. "He lost his grip on a big chunk of the tree." He pointed to it. "It fell on his leg. It may be broken."

"Oh dear," said Elizabeth. She looked around at the men.

"Well, someone must go for the doctor."

"In this snow?" said Mr. Marshall.

"Go on horseback, of course," said Elizabeth.

"Yes, quite," said Darcy, nodding. "And we must get Mr. Nelson inside."

"I'll go and fetch a blanket," said Elizabeth. "You can make a makeshift litter of that, carry him inside."

"Very good," said Darcy, nodding at her.

* * *

Darcy squeezed Nelson's hand. "Steady there, man, you' ll be all right."

Nelson looked up at him. "I'm really fine. Perhaps if I stood up."

Darcy shook his head at him. Nelson had not seen his leg yet, and that was by Darcy's design. He knew what it was like to look down at one's body and to see things twisting unnaturally. It was a dizzying sort of knowledge to have, and it only made things more difficult.

When Darcy had seen his own leg so badly mangled, he had been affected by it. Georgiana had been yelling for him, and it took him a bit of time to get himself together, to move, to drag himself down to her.

By then it had been too late.

Perhaps if he hadn't seen…

But no, because then he might have tried to stand, and that would never have worked. Nelson must not try it either.

"Just lie back," said Darcy. "We'll have you inside soon enough." He looked up and there was Elizabeth coming out of the house with Mrs. Peters and Nelson's sweetheart. He wondered if that was a good idea.

Miss Jennings was a kitchen maid, a young and pretty thing. What would she do when she saw Nelson's injury?

But when the women arrived, they were all business, seemingly less shaken by the events than some of the men, and Elizabeth took charge, instructing everyone how to move Nelson onto the blanket she'd brought.

120

"You, Mr. Darcy, stand back," said Elizabeth.

"I can help," he said.

She shook her head. "No, not with your leg. You've done quite enough already, come back here."

He did as she told him, and he had to admit he liked this side of her. She was so self-assured and strong. Perhaps he had misjudged her. Perhaps she was not quite as fragile as he might have thought.

They got Mr. Nelson inside and laid him out on a couch near the fire. He was given a great many cups of whisky, because he was now in some pain.

But he did not cry out or moan, perhaps because he didn't want to look weak in front of his sweetheart. She stayed at his side, keeping up a steady chatter of cheerfulness, telling him that he would be right as rain once the doctor arrived.

When the doctor did come, Nelson'd had so much whisky that he had passed out, and only woke when the doctor set the bone.

Then he did cry out, but only once.

Darcy stood in the corner, away from it all, watching, and trying very hard not to think about Georgiana's crying for help when he was helpless to get to her.

* * *

"And this is Mrs. Darcy," Mrs. Peters said, introducing Elizabeth to the doctor. "She was most helpful this afternoon."

"Why, that's very good indeed," said the doctor, smiling at Elizabeth. "It wouldn't be anything to be ashamed of if the lady of the house needed to retire to be away from such unpleasantness."

"It is only a broken leg," said Elizabeth. "I cannot think it would be too much for me."

"Well, if you are at all versed in dealing with Mr. Darcy, I should say not," said the doctor. "You know, his leg was not well mended."

"No?" said Elizabeth.

"His injuries were great," said the doctor, "and there were many things to care for. I don't think he was a good patient either. I cannot blame the doctor who cared for him entirely, but I will say that it could have been set much better."

"Oh," said Elizabeth, searching for Darcy in the room, feeling sympathy for him, yet again.

"Indeed, it could be corrected," said the doctor.

She turned to him. "Corrected? How?"

"Well, it would be agonizing for him," said the doctor. "It would mean rebreaking the leg and then setting it aright so that it would heal properly. But then he might likely do without his cane and be in quite a great deal less pain in the long run. I have mentioned it to him before. He refuses. I think it is less about the immediate agony, and more about some idea that he should suffer indefinitely. I believe he blames himself for his sister's death."

Elizabeth raised her eyebrows. "Well, you do not mince words, sir."

"I find it best to come right to the point," said the doctor. "I am well-versed in mending mens' bodies, but I cannot say I know what to do about their spirits. But perhaps you, his wife, you could convince him to let me mend the leg. He might listen to you."

"To me? Oh, I don't think so." Elizabeth sighed.

"Well, try," said the doctor, giving her an encouraging nod. "Nothing lost if he says no, after all?"

"True," she said. "Is there anything else that can be done for his pain?"

"He refuses laudanum," said the doctor.

"No, I know," she said.

"And perhaps he is right to do so," said the doctor. "It can be quite a thing to stop after one has started."

"But he seems to drink liquor so much," said Elizabeth. "I don't know if it's that much better in the end."

"Ah, true," said the doctor. "There are demons in many bottles, are there not? Well, you could try massaging some of the scar tissue."

"Massaging it?"

"Yes, in a hot bath," said the doctor. "It may help ease the pain a bit. I have given some instruction to his valet, but apparently Mr. Darcy is resistant."

She sighed again.

The doctor winked. "Men may let their wives touch them in ways they will not allow their valets, though, madam."

And Elizabeth blushed, her face getting quite hot.

CHAPTER FIFTEEN

Darcy stood in the doorway. "I don't seem to recall having ordered a bath."

"No," said Elizabeth, who was standing next to the tub. "That was me. I did that." She felt nervous about it all, but she thought she must try to talk to him. If he was keeping himself in pain when he did not need to, that was madness too. The pain seemed to drive his foul temper. Easing it might make things better for everyone in the household.

He stepped into the room. "Very forward of you."

"Well, I am your wife," she said.

"Not for much longer," he said, furrowing his brow.

She licked her lips. "About that..." Then she shook her head. "No, let us not speak of any of that now. That is not important. Please, come here. You needn't remove all your clothing. You may keep your smalls on. But do get in the bath, if you please."

"Bathe here? With you?"

"I have had a conversation with the doctor, and he recommended hot baths and massage for your pain."

Darcy raised his eyebrows. "Well, well, I see you're insistent on poking your nose where it doesn't belong."

She raised her chin. "He also says that he could mend your leg if you would allow him to break it again, and to set it aright, but you will not allow it."

"Have you ever broken a bone? It's rather painful, you know. It's not an experience I want to repeat."

"He says that once it healed, you would no longer need

124

your cane, and that it would alleviate a great deal of your persistent hurting."

"Perhaps," said Darcy.

"But you wish to stay in pain," said Elizabeth. "It's some sort of penance?"

He sighed.

"Did you mean to visit the penance upon me? Upon every member of this household?"

His lips thinned. At once, he crossed the room to the bath, moving quickly. When he got there, he divested himself of his jacket and waistcoat in moments. He began to untie his cravat. "So, you want to bathe me, then?"

"I want to help you not feel pain," she said. "I think it is the pain that drives you to be so cruel."

He yanked off his cravat and pulled his shirt over his head, not bothering to unbutton it.

She swallowed, unnerved at the sight of his bare chest, which she had not ever seen. He was scarred there, too. The line of it traveled down over his collar, over his chest, fading out only above his belly. But he was also powerful and muscled and... well, rather pleasant to look at.

He gave her a wide smile, noticing her discomfort and enjoying it. "This is what you wished, is it not?" He unbuttoned his trousers and pushed them off.

Her eyes widened.

He was not wearing any smalls. He was entirely naked beneath his trousers, and she could see everything, including his male part, which was...

She had seen male parts on statues before, and his seemed wrong in some way. It was rather too large, and it was sticking out of his body in an odd and somewhat frightening way.

She was so caught up in staring at it that she almost didn't at first see the other mass of scar tissue, at the top of his leg. It was pink and ugly and painful to even look at.

"Oh, Mr. Darcy!" she cried out when she saw it. "It must

be *that* which needs massaging."

"I can think of a number of things I wouldn't mind your massaging," he said in a very deep voice.

Her face went red again.

He climbed into the bath. "Did I say that I wasn't going to apologize to you anymore?"

"Why aren't you wearing any smalls?"

"I suppose I should apologize anyway. I don't know what I'm about. I thought to scandalize you, I suppose, scare you away with my nakedness. But you don't scare easily, do you, madam?"

She cleared her throat. "Well, I must say that your, er, member is a bit frighteningly formed."

He laughed, delighted, surprised. "What?"

She was blushing again. "I don't think it's supposed to... stand up in that manner."

He laughed again, throwing back his head, sliding down in the bath so that his face was nearly submerged.

"Why are you laughing?" she said. "And really, you should allow me to massage the area that is hurt. I don't even know why we're continuing this conversation."

He stopped laughing and simply grinned at her. "It probably shouldn't be standing up, in fact. It's entirely a compliment to you."

"I don't understand." She shook her head.

"That's good," he said. "If you are so wide-eyed with your fortune-seeking husband, he'll be quite convinced of your innocence."

She looked away.

He was quiet.

"Let me help you," she whispered. "Let me ease the pain."

"You don't need to bother with me, Elizabeth," he said. "You will be gone soon enough."

Her first name on his lips did strange things to her insides. The fact that he was naked was similarly disconcerting. She could see part of his chest uncovered in the water, his strong arms. She felt out of sorts.

"I appreciate what you're trying to do," he continued gently, "but I don't deserve it. And look at how I've taken this sweet gesture you've made toward me and turned it vulgar. You are good, Elizabeth, but don't waste anymore of your goodness on me. Go and read before bed, relax after this difficult day we've had."

She knelt down so that she was eye level with him. That was a bit better. She could no longer see so much of his bare skin. "I think you're simply trying to avoid feeling better."

"I will enjoy the bath on my own," he said. "I promise."

"I think you're afraid of letting me help you."

He drew in a shuddering breath, looking at her. "You don't know what you're asking. You want to massage my upper thigh?"

"If that's where it hurts, then yes."

"No." He shut his eyes, letting out another laugh, but this one was wild and high-pitched. When he opened his eyes, he shook his head at her. "No."

"Why not? Because I would see your weakness and you would —"

"Because you are leaving me, and I am going to turn you over to some other man, and you do not belong to me anymore. It would be ... improper ... to allow such intimacy."

"You've never given a fig for propriety since I've known you, Mr. Darcy."

"Elizabeth..."

"You keep doing that," she said, and her voice wavered a bit.

"What?" His voice was barely more than a whisper.

" Calling me by my first name. Shall I call you Fitzwilliam?"

His jaw twitched.

"Fitzwilliam, I am going to reach across the bath and put

my hands under the water, and—"

"No, you are not."

She reached over the side of the tub.

He grasped her wrists. "Leave me." He was begging her.

"Let go of me," she said. "It doesn't have to be improper unless you make it improper."

He laughed that wild laugh again.

"Aren't you at least curious to see if it would, in fact, ease some of the pain?"

He went slack, his grip on her wrists loosening. "You're not going to leave, are you?"

"I can be rather stubborn, Fitzwilliam. Perhaps you didn't know this about me."

"No, I think I did," he said quietly, looking up at her. "Your stubbornness is my favorite thing about you." Then he shook his head. "No, that's not true. My favorite thing about you is the way you say 'Fitzwilliam.'"

A thrill went through her. This *was* intimate. This was... She licked her lips. "I'm not leaving you." She thrust her hands under the water.

"Yes, we established that," he said.

"No, I mean, I'm not leaving Pemberley. I'm not going home. I'm staying here. I'm staying married to you."

"You don't mean that."

Her fingers brushed his skin under the water.

He gasped.

What had she just touched?

He made a funny noise and then he grasped her hands again, but not to stop her, to move her. He guided her fingers through the water, and then she felt the smooth lumps of scars against her palms. "Oh," she breathed.

He swallowed, his Adam's apple bobbing. He leaned his head back to expose his neck to her, and it was beautiful. *He* was beautiful.

She explored the scars, gentle, careful, her fingers finding the edges of them.

128

He shut his eyes.

She did not know what she was doing. How to massage? How much pressure? Should she gather up his flesh in her hands? She was afraid to push too hard, so she only rubbed, her fingers gliding through the water.

He made a humming noise, something on the edge of pain and satisfaction.

She stopped moving. "Does it hurt?"

"A little," he murmured. "But don't stop. It's good."

So, she didn't. She massaged, gentle and hesitant, for a very long time, until her fingers cramped, and then she stopped, sinking down to sit next to the bath.

She was soaked, somehow. Water had traveled down her sleeves to the bodice of her dress. The floor was wet. It was soaking through her skirts.

He moved. She could hear the water gurgling around him.

She lifted her gaze to find his.

He reached a wet hand out of the bath to cup her cheek. "Elizabeth..."

She leaned into his touch. It sent warm rivers of sensation through her.

"Why are you good to me?"

She covered his hand with her own, holding it against her cheek. She could feel that his fingers were wrinkled from being submerged in the water, and that made her smile, and it made her feel close to him in away she hadn't before.

"I'm not a good man," he said.

She opened her eyes. "Maybe you should try to be one." She turned her face, pressed her lips into his palm.

He groaned.

She leaned closer, her face closer to his. She wanted to kiss his lips again. This time she wouldn't run away.

"All right," he breathed. "If I were a good man, I would make you leave me."

"Fitzwilliam—"

129

"Go," he said, his voice growing harsh. "I mean it, leave me."

"No, I won't—"

"You will." He nodded at her. "The snow will melt, and you will go. Back to your home, back to your family, and far away from all of this. You will be better off without me."

CHAPTER SIXTEEN

When Darcy awoke the next morning, his leg did not hurt. Elizabeth had been right that heat and the massage were good for the pain. He had not been so completely without pain in a long time, and he lay under the covers, staring up at the ceiling, unsure of how to proceed.

The pain was like a haze that settled over everything, and without it, he found himself musing over impossible things.

She'd said she wanted to stay.

Why would she say such a thing? It made no sense. She couldn't want to stay. She couldn't want to be with him. He tried to think of one single good thing he'd done for her, and he came up completely empty. Perhaps she'd said it only out of fear. Even with money, a woman whose marriage had been annulled had a certain status in society. It would not be easy for her.

But surely, she must see that it would be easier than being here with him. He was a man drowning in pain and grief.

Except it didn't hurt right now, and he allowed himself to imagine it for several long moments. He imagined it just as she said, Elizabeth at his side as they hosted balls and dinner parties. He thought of her dancing, her laughing, her eyes catching the lights as she moved...

She could be his, truly his.

He thought of her next him in his bed.

She would have let me bed her last night, he thought. God, he'd wanted her. The experience had been almost tortuously erotic. Certainly, it had some health benefits as well, but her hands on his skin, so close to him… He'd been so hard he thought he might explode.

And she was so innocent. So sweet. So…

Oh, Lord, he wanted her. He wanted her to be his, and he wanted her by his side while he slowly cleared out Georgiana's rooms for their own children to take up residence in that nursery. He thought if she was there, he might be able to manage it. Maybe he could tell her about Georgiana, talk about his sister without the pain bubbling up in him and threatening to drown him in its torrent.

Maybe…

But hadn't this all gone on long enough?

Hadn't he done enough to Elizabeth? Shouldn't he let her be, at long last?

He got out of bed and half-dressed himself without his valet, only because he was amazed at his range of movement without pain. Perhaps a hot bath every night would nearly banish the pain. Perhaps she was right, and he was keeping himself in pain as a sort of penance for his many sins.

But she was right that his pain made him horrid, and he took it out on his staff and his friends and on her as well.

He needed to consider that others didn't need to suffer.

His valet came to help him finish dressing and then he went down to breakfast, where Elizabeth was already pouring herself a cup of chocolate.

He looked at her, and all he could do was smile. He gazed at her, the silly smile on his face, and everything slowed down.

She turned to look at him. She smiled too. "Mr. Darcy. You're looking well this morning."

"Yes," he said. "I am loathe to admit it, of course, but your ministrations seemed to have been most effective."

"Truly? Is the pain less?"

"A great deal less."

132

"Then you must let me to do it again then," she said.

He let out something between a gasp and a laugh. "You…" He cleared his throat. "Well, I'm sure you'll soon be on your way. The snow must be melting."

"It's not, in fact," she said. "A wind has come in, and it's drifting badly. Haven't you looked out the windows this morning?"

"I have not," he said. "Snow drifts, you say?"

"High as a horse in some places," she said. "Looks as though you're stuck with me."

"Oh, well, somehow I'll muddle on," he said, winking at her.

Her smile widened and her cheeks flushed, and his heart hurt because she was so beautiful. "I wish you wouldn't keep talking about sending me away. I don't think you can force me, after all. You did marry me. You can't toss me aside at a whim."

"Well, I don't think that's strictly true," he said. "I probably could do exactly that, if I really made up my mind to do it."

"*If* you made your mind? Then you have not done so?"

"I mean to," he said. "I mean to, but you make it all so very difficult to be a good man, Mrs. Darcy."

"Oh?" She laughed. "How is that?"

He reached out and brushed her cheek.

She sighed, closing her eyes. "I think there are a great many ways that you could be a good man that don't involve getting rid of me."

"Well, you're wrong," he said. "Keeping you here is selfish and cruel to you."

"You ought to let me decide that for myself."

"You seem to have gone rather mad, madam, pardon me for saying so."

She opened her eyes. "Yes, I think I may have." She laughed again. "I don't know what it is about you." And then she closed the distance between them and put her lips on his, like it was nothing, like they kissed over breakfast every morning.

* * *

" Did I ruin your dresses, then? " Darcy was looking through Elizabeth's wardrobe.

She was sitting on her bed, watching him, feeling just as mad as he had accused her of being. She had made up her mind to leave already, and changing her mind was folly. She was not the sort of woman to fall for a man like this. Why had she fallen for him? Because he wanted her?

What a stupid bit of vanity on her part.

"I had them mended," she said.

"Oh, good," he said.

"Some are still being mended," she said. "Even now, as we speak."

"I see," he said. "I am very sorry for what I did to your clothes. It's unpardonable."

"It is," she said. "Quite."

"You shouldn't forgive me for it."

"I know that," she said. "Who says that I have?

" Ah, " he said, inclining his head. " Perhaps you have not." He turned away from the wardrobe to peer at her on the bed. " What am I doing in here? Why have I followed you into your bedroom? I should go."

"Don't," she said. She patted the space next to her on the bed. "Sit with me."

He hesitated, and then he did it. He sat quite close to her. Their shoulders brushed.

She peered at him. He was looking straight ahead, and in profile, she couldn't see the scars on his face. She wondered what it would have been like to have met him before he had lost his sister, before he had been hurt.

"I should go," he said again.

"Perhaps," she murmured.

He stood up.

She stood up too. "Fitzwilliam?"

"Don't call me that."

"Do you think that if I did forgive you, you would let me?"

He furrowed his brow. "What do you mean by that?"

"Could you let it all go? Could you try to be happy, to be..." She cocked her head. "What horrible sin is it that you've committed that you don't think you deserve forgiveness for anyway? *Did* you kill that man, that Wickham?"

He grimaced, and his voice was tight. "For heaven's sake, must you say his name?"

"Did you?"

"No," he said. "But if I had, I certainly wouldn't feel guilty about it."

She regarded him, unsure what she thought of that answer. She tried to fathom the idea of having killed a person and being glad of it. She couldn't. Of course, Mr. Darcy had said that he *hadn't* killed Mr. Wickham. Could she believe him? "Well, then... what is it?"

He shook his head. "I'm going." He started towards the door.

She caught him by the sleeve of his jacket. "Whatever it is, could you let it go? Could you try to be happy with me?"

He caught her gaze with his own and then he looked away, studying his feet. "I... want to be happy with you, Elizabeth. I don't know if I can even explain how much I want it."

"So, then, you're saying—"

"But I don't know if I'm capable of it." He pulled his arm away from her. "I don't know if it's something I could ever let go. The evidence of it all is permanently etched into my face, do you understand?"

She reached up and caressed his scars.

"Don't do that." His voice wasn't strong.

She kissed him again.

He offered only token resistance, and then he gave himself over to the kiss. He caught her about the waist and pulled her body against his.

They kissed in a fury, like the wind that raged outside the windows.

She felt as if she was being torn apart by it, as though it was too much for her to handle, as though it might break her. And yet, all she wanted was more of his mouth and more of his hands on her, and she urged his fingers higher on her back, telling him to unbutton her dress.

He sighed, his mouth on hers, and he did as she asked. His fingers worked at her neck, one button at a time, and they kissed and kissed and kissed.

She seized handfuls of his shirt and pulled them out of where they were tucked into his trousers. She put her hands under the fabric, flat against the warmth of his stomach.

He grunted. He tugged on her dress.

She pulled her arms out of the sleeves, revealing her stays and her shift beneath. Her heart started to beat wildly. This was happening.

He looked her over, his gaze traveling greedily over what she'd uncovered. His fingers came up slowly and deliberately. He brushed his thumb over her neck, traced a path down to her collarbone.

And the door opened, and Meg's voice came in cheerily. "There's a letter for you, mum. Imagine, delivering letters in this wind and snow. I can't understand what must have possessed the—"

She had seen them.

Mr. Darcy moved, turning and placing his body between her and Meg, blocking Elizabeth from view, though it was silly, wasn't it, since Meg was the one who helped Elizabeth dress and undress?

Meg looked terrified. "Oh, I did not realize... It's the middle of the morning, and—"

"It's all right." Elizabeth felt the need to reassure her. "Leave the letter on my desk."

"Yes, mum." Meg curtsied, trying to look everywhere

except at them. "I'm sorry, mum." She dropped the letter on the desk and fairly fled out of the room.

When the door closed, Elizabeth felt a giggle escaping her lips.

But Mr. Darcy wasn't laughing. He rubbed his forehead, and he sucked in a breath.

Elizabeth felt the laughter die in her throat. "What's the matter? It's not as if she truly saw anything, and there is nothing to be ashamed of. We are husband and wife, and —"

"Turn around," said Mr. Darcy.

"Why?" she said, but she obeyed.

"Put your arms back in the sleeves. I'll button you back up, unless you'd like to call for Meg."

"Mr. Darcy, I..." She glanced over her shoulder at his expression, and she decided not to continue. She obeyed him wordlessly. His fingers were deft, quickly doing up all the buttons.

When he was done, he tucked in his shirt and started across the room.

"You're leaving, then?" she said.

He reached the door and opened it. "When I kissed you at the ball, it felt like this. Wanting you... it motivates me to take things from you that I shouldn't. I won't anymore. I promised I wouldn't, and I have to be strong."

* * *

Darcy cut his meat at the table. "Who was the letter from?"

"It was from Jane, of course," she said.

"Ah, yes, you do seem to get a great many letters from your sister," said Darcy. "You are quite close."

"We promised before I left that we would write each other daily, in order to stay close, so that we might know all the minutia of each other's lives. That way, it would be almost as if we were still under the same roof."

"I see," he said, smiling.

"It's not so easy, though," said Elizabeth. "She has many

137

things to write to me about, but I..."

"Well, I suppose it's boring for you here," he said.

"No," she said. "I wouldn't describe my life here as boring, not when you are so difficult to predict.'

"Yes, I see," he said. "There's always the chance that I shall fly into a rage, then?"

She stabbed at a boiled potato with her fork. "Well, I don't write to her about those."

"No?"

"I... I suppose I don't want her to worry," she said.

"And she would, if she knew what it was like living with a monster like me?"

"I wouldn't call you that." But she was looking at the potato on her fork, not at him.

He sighed. His voice was gentle. "I can't help but think you are deceiving yourself, Elizabeth. You think that perhaps you can change me, but that is a fool's errand. I am too broken for that. You oughtn't embroil yourself in all this. If your sister would worry about you, then I think you know the truth of what it is between you and me. You should not tempt..." He shook his head, and the bottom went out of his voice. "I would beg you not to kiss me again."

She didn't say anything.

It was quiet for some time.

Elizabeth put the potato in her mouth. Chewed. Swallowed. She washed it down with a drink of wine. "Jane and Mr. Bingley have set the date for their wedding. We are invited to go."

"Oh," he said. "When is it?"

"Two weeks hence, but she says that we may come as soon as we are able. I can help with the preparations."

He nodded. "Good. As soon as the snow clears, you'll go."

"And you, sir?"

"I shan't go. You will go alone. I have said that I shall release you from this marriage, and I shall. There's no time like the present."

She looked up at him, and he could see she'd been hurt by what he'd said.

"Come now, Elizabeth," he said softly, "you must see that it's the right thing. You are too good for this place, too good for me, and I will not transgress further against you. I have already taken far more than I should have from you. I may never be able to make it right, but I must do what I can."

She swallowed, and her lower lip was trembling. She opened her mouth to speak, but then seemed overcome.

"You know it's madness to be with me."

She turned back to her plate, sniffing. "Yes."

He let out a breath, relieved.

"Madness," she whispered. "I lie about you to Jane. I am frightened of you sometimes." A long, long pause. "Yes." She nodded. "I will go."

"It's the best thing for you," he said. "We both know it."

CHAPTER SEVENTEEN

Darcy had to put Elizabeth off the idea of any further massage by having his valet assist him. He had the bath drawn and assured her he would be all right without her help.

Then he submitted to the ministrations of his valet, and he had to admit that the massage wasn't nearly as distracting without Elizabeth's hands on him. It might even have been better at alleviating his pain. Or perhaps it was only that his muscles were loosened after having been worked at the night before.

Whatever the case, he didn't feel the need for his nightly strong drink by the fire. He felt afflicted with restless energy, instead, and he prowled the house without his cane.

Outside, the winds had not stopped, but the temperature had raised, and he heard the distant rumbling of thunder. That was good, then. The wind would blow in the warmer storm, and the rain would wash away the snow, and Elizabeth could leave.

The thought went through him like a hot lance of pain.

He didn't want to let her go.

No, of course I don't, and that is why I must. I have been nothing but selfish and cruel to her. I must set her free.

He found himself in the east wing of the house, and he went into the nursery, which had been his own nursery as well, when he had been small. Some of the toys here had been his toys before they were Georgiana's.

Not the dolls, though.

He remembered when she had been so in love with these dolls. Each had names and detailed histories, and she would sit on his knee and chatter to him in a little-girl voice that somehow sounded so grown-up.

He wondered if it hadn't been a curse that they were so far apart in age. Losing their parents, it had cast him in a nearly fatherly role toward her, and he had been blind to the fact that she was growing up.

Her childhood, it had been his comfort in the wake of their parents' loss. She had been young and sweet and small and some part of him had never wanted that to change. He wanted her to remain a little girl forever. He wanted her to sit on his knee and chatter about dolls.

But she had been becoming a young woman, and Darcy hadn't seen.

Wickham had.

Damn that man.

Outside, the thunder crashed, closer now, and lightning lit up the windows.

Startled by the noise, he stood up.

There was a figure illuminated in the doorway.

He let out a little cry. For a moment, he thought it was Georgiana herself.

But in an instant, he knew he was wrong. The figure was too tall, and the hair was the wrong color. The long white sleeping gown, though, that had thrown him.

It was Elizabeth.

He made his way across the room towards her.

"I'm sorry," she said. "I know I shouldn't have come here, but I wanted to remember it. I couldn't sleep, and I won't be living here anymore, and I wanted to look at it all again and try to commit it to my memory."

"It's all right," he said, his voice hoarse. "You may go anywhere you please. I was wrong to keep you out of here."

"I'll go back to bed now," she said. She didn't move.

He stopped directly in front of her.

Lightning flashed outside again. More thunder. It was frightfully loud.

Elizabeth cringed.

He put his arm around her without thinking about it.

She leaned into him, and it was as if she fit there, *belonged* there.

He drew in a breath and it made noise when he expelled it. "She was very angry with me toward the end. I kept her up here in the nursery, and she was fifteen years old. To me, that still seemed very young, but to her, she thought she was on the edge of womanhood. She was cross with me. She begged for freedom, and the more she begged, the more I tamped down on her."

Elizabeth looked up at him. "Well, she was young. What freedom could she have had?"

"Your own sister, the youngest one, when did she make her debut into society?"

"Oh, well, Lydia, she's always been old for her age." Elizabeth waved this away.

"Perhaps Georgiana was too, and I just refused to see it," said Darcy.

"Did she do something?" said Elizabeth. "Did she try to rebel against your strictness?"

Darcy nodded.

"Is that what caused the carriage accident?"

Lightning flashed brightly, followed closely on its heels by another crash of thunder. And then the rain began to pelt the windows.

Elizabeth looked up at him. "I'm sorry. I know you don't like to talk about it."

"She wanted to go on a trip," he said. "I didn't want her to go. I thought she was too young to travel on her own, but she wore me down. She enlisted the help of her governess, Miss Younge, who I thought was a trustworthy woman, but who did not, in fact, have Georgiana's best interests at heart. They both wrote to me, telling me that there was nothing to fear, only a lark. I believed them, and I didn't think anything was amiss. A week later, a letter reached me from Mr. Wickham, telling me that he and my sister were married and demanding to be given the full sum of her dowry."

Elizabeth pulled away from him, horrified. " What? Married?"

He pushed past her, into the hallway. At the end of the hallway, rain lashed the window pane and a ghostly pale light drifted through it. The air seemed heavy, as if it had absorbed the weight of the water coming from the clouds outside.

"But did she know?" said Elizabeth. "Did she want to marry him? Did she deceive you or was she taken in by him?"

"Wickham was a childhood friend," said Darcy. "He was the son of my father's steward, but my father took a liking to him, raised him like one of his own children. Did everything he could for him, even sent him to school along with me. Wickham and I were once close, but he proved to be a careless sort of man. Money would flow through his fingers like water, and it was all he cared about."

"Oh, dear," said Elizabeth. "So, he came after your sister, then?"

" That was my fault," said Darcy. " You see, my father had wanted Wickham to take over the parsonage here in Derbyshire. He wanted to provide for him by giving him an occupation. But after my father's death, when the position became open, Wickham wasn't interested. He asked me if I could not give him the value of the living instead. I thought it was probably a bad idea, but I also didn't think he would do very will as a clergyman. I knew he wouldn't be able to handle the money. I *knew* it. I gave it to him anyway."

"I don't see how that's your fault," said Elizabeth.

"Well, he went through it rather more quickly than even I had feared, and he came back for more money."

"And you refused him?"

"No, I didn't." Darcy dragged a hand over his face. "No, that first time, I didn't. He was in a bad spot, and he said he would go to debtors' prison without it, and he asked if I could bear to have his suffering on my conscience, and I gave in."

"Well, then, why ...?" Elizabeth sighed. "Because he came back again, and that time you did refuse him."

"Yes," said Darcy. "I told him he must face consequences for his actions at some point. He was angry with me. He vowed to my face that he would make me sorry. And he did." He grimaced. "The letter he sent me about Georgiana, it was, er, full of detail about things he had... it was vulgar. It was..." He shut his eyes as if shutting them could make him unsee the words, the images they'd conjured. "He seemed to delight in the idea that he'd hurt her." His voice broke. "He knew that hurting her was the best way to hurt me."

Elizabeth was aghast. "That... nothing about that is your fault. What should you have done, given him more money?"

"I would have, had I known what he planned to do. When I got there and I found her, she was..." He walked away, trying to walk all that away too, sinking his hands into his hair. "He had forced himself on her and beaten her and she..."

Elizabeth was behind him, her hands on his back. "Fitzwilliam..."

"We fought," said Darcy. "I hit him with my fists. I should have shot him. I don't know why I didn't come there with a loaded pistol. I... I wasn't thinking. I've never been so distraught... He knocked me down." He turned to look at Elizabeth.

Elizabeth's lips parted.

"He had beaten her with his fists, and he beat me too, and I was bested by that wretch." He'd never said it aloud. Saying it aloud made the shame fresh again. His nostrils flared. "He took her in the carriage, and they were leaving. I got myself together and went after them on horseback. I'm the one who caused the carriage to go over the cliff."

"I'm sure you didn't—"

"I was trying to save her, but I bungled that too, and I killed her."

"*No.*" She lifted her chin. "Don't say that."

"You weren't there," he said, his voice rising. "You don't know what—"

"You loved your sister. You didn't kill her. No matter what happened, moment by moment, it was that awful man Wickham that did it. I'm glad you killed him."

"I *didn't* kill him," he said, letting out a bitter laugh. "He got away."

"But Mrs. Hurst said that there are rumors. No one's seen him since, so people think—"

"I saw him climbing up over that cliff," he said. "He got away. If he's hiding, well, that's likely because he knows that if I find him, I *will* kill him." He searched her expression, wanting to see how she'd react to that declaration.

Thunder crashed and lightning lit up her face, and he didn't think he'd ever seen a woman more beautiful.

She kissed him.

He tried to pull away from her.

He wanted to think he tried, anyway.

* * *

Elizabeth panted. Her body seemed to be convulsing in time with the thunder outside, but now they were both retreating—the crashes outside and the wild pleasure that had seized her and rippled through her, turning her inside out.

Her sleeping gown was up at her armpits and her body was bare.

Fitzwilliam was inside her. He was panting too. His fingers were between their bodies, touching her where her thighs met. That was what he'd done right before it had happened—whatever it was—the burst of rippling pleasure.

She touched his face, the side of his face that wasn't marred with scars, touched him because she needed to see that he was real. Everything seemed unreal just then, and she was afraid she might lose herself.

He shuddered against her, a groan escaping his lips, digging the fingers of one of his hands into her hip.

She gasped.

Then he was still. He brought his face down, resting his forehead against hers.

They breathed together.

He was half-undressed as well. He didn't have his jacket or his vest or his cravat or his trousers, but he still wore his shirt. It was partially unbuttoned. Or... some of the buttons might have been ripped off.

She wasn't sure.

Everything had been strange.

He had been so overcome by that horrible memory, and his sadness and pain and shame had risen up in the air along with the storm, like something alive. She hadn't been able to bear it. She'd thought to... to comfort him, somehow, but when they touched, it wasn't comfort.

It was...

Oh, she didn't know. It was as if the madness that had taken over her, that made her want him at all, had crested like the snow drifts, and she had been buried in that insanity.

But it had been good, even sweet, a ferocious sweetness. Now that it had passed, she only wanted to cling to him. Her lips sought his again and he obliged her. They kissed slowly, thoroughly, softly.

He let out a low groan, breaking the kiss. His body slipped out of hers. He buried his face in the crook of her neck and shoulder. "Ah, Elizabeth, I'm so sorry."

"Why?" she whispered, reaching up to stroke his hair. "You needn't be sorry. I was told it would hurt, and there would be blood, but it didn't. There wasn't. It was... rather lovely."

He was boneless against her, exhausted, wrung out. "How do I send you away now?"

"You don't," she whispered.

"Everything I touch, I destroy," he muttered.

"I'm not destroyed," she replied.

He pulled away, studying her face.

"I want..." She reached for him. "I want you to hold me. I want to be close to you. Please."

"Elizabeth..."

"It's dreadfully cold up here, isn't it?" She shivered. It was funny how she hadn't noticed before.

He stood up and stepped back into his trousers. He offered her his hand. He helped her up. He put his arm around her and she put her head on his shoulder. They walked out of the east wing together.

He took them to his bedchamber, and they climbed under the blankets together.

She fell asleep in the circle of his arms.

* * *

It was dawn, white dawn, when Elizabeth woke to the sounds of low male whispering.

She opened her eyes, at first disoriented because she did not know where she was. But then she remembered the events of the evening before, that she was in Mr. Darcy's bed.

The knowledge swelled up inside her, a sweet echo of what had passed between them the night before. She had thought herself in love with him before, but perhaps she hadn't understood love then. Now...

Oh, Lord, now the feelings she felt for him had grown so large she wondered at her body's ability to contain them.

She sat up in bed, and Mr. Darcy shut the door, closing out his valet. He crossed the room to his wardrobe and took out clothing. When he turned, he realized she was awake.

"Oh," he said. "I didn't mean to wake you."

She yawned. "Can you not come back to bed? I must admit it was warmer with you in it."

He gave her a sad smile. "I, er, I have to go. I have just received news of some important business I need to attend to."

"Go? You mean leave Pemberley?"

"Yes, it's rather urgent. I'm afraid I have to leave at once."

"What is this urgent business? Can't you wait until after my sister's wedding?"

He shook his head. "No, no. I have thought it over, and there is no reason why we can't proceed as we were. Go home to your family, and I will grant you an annulment."

"What?" She sat up straight. "But we can't get an annulment. We have ... " She gestured, searching for the word. "Consummated," she settled on. "Consummated things. Thoroughly."

"Yes," he said, not meeting her gaze. "But no one knows that."

She was aghast. "No. Please, don't do this to me. Fitzwilliam, I love you."

He looked up at her, his eyes wide in shock. He let out a sort of strangled noise. "You don't mean that. You can't love a man like me. You said yourself you were frightened of me."

She thought of something. "What if I'm with child?" She flung it out like a gauntlet.

He cleared his throat. "It was only once. It's not likely."

"But it's possible, isn't it?"

"Yes." He nodded.

"So, you see, you can't."

He licked his lips. "No, of course, we'll wait. A few weeks and we should know, yes?"

She thought about it. It was likely sooner than that. Next week she was due for her monthly time. But she only nodded, confirming it.

"So, go home, go to your sister's wedding. You may find that once you're away from me, it's easier."

"It won't be," she said.

"If there is a child, of course, there is no question..." He swallowed. " But still, perhaps there is no need for us to remain together here in this house. I have a home in London. You could bring one or two of your sisters to stay with you —"

"Why?" She thrust aside the covers and got out of bed. "Why are you being this way? I know you felt it, too."

"Felt what?" His face twisted.

"When we were together, it was —"

"What? When I tupped you?" He gazed at her evenly. " Yes, I wanted you, madam. I tore your life to shreds because of it, and now I've had you. It's done." He turned on his heel and walked out of the room, leaving her there alone.

CHAPTER EIGHTEEN

The snow had been washed away by the rain the night before, but there was mud to contend with, so it was three days before she could leave for Hertfordshire.

She sent a letter home, telling them of her arrival, making excuses for her husband, saying that he had business to attend to that could not wait. She pretended to be cheery about it all, even though she was in turmoil.

She had asked him why, but after he left, she had mused over it all, and it was clear to her.

He had said it to her afterward.

Everything I touch, I destroy.

In some stupid way, he fancied that he was being noble. He thought that he hurt her, and he thought that all he *would* do was hurt her. He hated himself for failing his sister. He blamed himself for her suffering, for her death.

Truly, it did sound as if his sister had been tormented. What an awful thing to happen to a young girl. It broke Elizabeth's heart.

She understood him, but he was being an idiot, and she wouldn't accept it. No, they were married, and they had come together, and she loved him. And what was more, though he hadn't said it, he loved her too.

Or...

Well, he at least cared about her. If he hadn't cared, he wouldn't be trying to send her away. He was doing that to protect her. That was his stupid nobility.

Anyway, she wouldn't allow him to cast her off. If he

tried to get the marriage annulled, she would contradict him, swear that he'd had her over and over. She would not submit to this.

But then...

As she rode in the carriage back to Hertfordshire, she watched the scenery outside and she began to remember things. She remembered his sweeping all the plates off the table, the sound of them shattering on the floor, and the way he bared his teeth when he was angry. She remembered him dragging her down the stairs and throwing open the door to the swirling snow. She remembered his anger when she had ventured into the east wing. She remembered the way he had kissed her at the Netherfield Ball, forcing her to marry him, taking her choice from her.

She had long thought she was mad to love him.

Perhaps it would be wise to get away from him. It would do more than break her heart now, it would shatter it into a million pieces, but perhaps she would be better off with a broken heart than to be locked up in a house with him in a rage. What if he hurt her?

She had worried about a child before, and had determined there was no worry on that score, but now...

When she arrived at home, she wasn't sure of anything anymore.

She was glad of the noise in the home, the way that there was always someone talking or moving, and there wasn't so much time to think.

Her mother was all grand proclamations of Jane's beauty and Bingley's wealth. She would not stop talking about it, saying that she had known all along that Jane would make a good match and that there was nothing that would stand in the way of their having the happiest of marriages. She even took credit for introducing them, which everyone knew wasn't true.

Mary had decided to abandon playing the piano in favor of painting, and now the house was littered with various objects that Mary had set up as models for her still-life paintings. Which would have been fine if the fruit was not starting to smell.

Kitty took it upon herself to throw anything away she deemed to be rotting, which Mary took objection to, because she claimed it was ruining her paintings. The two girls got into loud arguments about it.

Jane would have usually kept the peace, separating the girls, but she was much too consumed with excitement over her wedding to even notice what was going on.

Lydia was surprisingly quiet, doing embroidery instead. Well, from what Elizabeth observed, she seemed to be dreamily gazing out into empty air over her embroidery, not actually doing any stitches.

Her father stayed in the sitting room amongst all this after her arrival, which wasn't like him. He tended to mutter about silly girls and take shelter in his study. "Lizzy, are you all right?" he said to her, settling in next to her on the couch.

"Perfectly fine, Papa." She smiled at him.

"That husband of yours hasn't come with you."

"No, it's as I said, he is engaged in important business."

Her father nodded, and he looked concerned. "Tell me the truth, Lizzy, has he ever done anything that would frighten you?"

She forced herself to laugh. "Papa, what a thing to say."

"Listen to me, my darling, I feel that I should not have allowed this marriage to go forward. You say the word, and I shall make it my personal business to keep you away from him. Even though you are married, it does not mean you need to reside under the same roof as he does. Why, as I'm sure you know, there are many married couples who live rather separate lives, and I am not above threatening that cur within an inch of his life—"

"Papa, no, I'm fine," she said.

But she wasn't sure he believed her.

* * *

Elizabeth had resolved not to talk of the truth of her relationship with Mr. Darcy with anyone.

But eventually, she found herself confessing all to Jane. Even though she was a married woman now, she and her sister had wanted nothing more than to share their old bed as they had from girlhood. And in the dark, both of them whispering while they faced each other, their heads on their respective pillows, it was somehow easier to say it all aloud.

Everything came spilling out, from his angry outbursts to his desire to have their marriage annulled.

"Annulled?" Jane was shocked. "But Lizzy, that would be the most villainous thing of all to do to you."

" He promises to give me a monetary settlement, something very large. Enough that I might, in his terms, attract some man with nothing but a title who is seeking a fortune," said Elizabeth.

"Oh," said Jane in a different voice.

" I don't think I would marry again, however, " said Elizabeth. "I would live on my own, I believe. I would own my own home. I would be rather like a widow, don't you think? Can you imagine the freedom?"

"I can see the appeal in that," said Jane. "No husband or father to tell you what to do. Belonging only to yourself. Having your own means to do as you will. Yes, I understand, Lizzy. I think it is the best outcome of your unfortunate situation. I can promise that Mr. Bingley and I will welcome you into our society. Fear nothing on that score."

" I do not fear anything. But I am not certain it is the future I will have."

"You cannot mean to want to stay in the marriage," said Jane. "After the way he tore your dresses and yelled at you? After the way he treated that poor Mrs. Peters, and all over a dog?"

" It wasn't about the dog, it was about Mr. Wickham. And Mr. Wickham has… has unmanned him. He *destroyed* Fitzwilliam, and —"

"That is no excuse for his behavior, I'm afraid," said Jane. "Why, he is a beast, Lizzy."

" There is also the slight chance that I might be ... " Elizabeth rolled over onto her back and stared at the ceiling.

"Might be what?"

"Carrying his child," Elizabeth whispered.

"What? But I thought you said an annulment."

Elizabeth sighed. " Yes, well, he said that no one else knows that… that we…"

"Oh, Lizzy, this man. He is so monstrous, I don't know what to do." Jane's voice wasn't strong. "I swear that I cannot see any good in him, and coming from me, that is saying something. How could he use you in that manner if he intended to cast you aside?"

She thought of his words. *Yes, I wanted you… and now I've had you. It is done.*

It couldn't really be that simple. He couldn't have married her only because he desired to bed her.

Could he?

"He says that if I am with child, of course we will remain married."

"Oh, how chivalrous of him." Jane's tone was sharp.

Elizabeth laughed softly. " I fear that I may… the main problem, Jane, as I see it, is that I love him."

"What?" Jane sat up in bed, staring down at her.

Elizabeth laughed again. " You think I have gone mad, don't you?"

"I confess I…" Jane plopped down on the bed next to her. "Why?"

"Why do I love him?"

"Yes."

"Why do you love Bingley?"

"Oh, that is not the same."

"I mean it. Why?"

"Well, because he is…" Jane sighed.

"You see, it is difficult to put it into words, is it not?"

"He is a good man," said Jane. "Bingley would never hurt me, and he would hurt anyone that tried to hurt me. If he knew that someone intended me harm, he would get me out of harm's way immediately."

"Yes, well, you see, I think that is why Mr. Darcy wishes to have our marriage annulled. To get me away from him and out of harm's way."

Jane was quiet.

"He cares about me, don't you see? Is it so strange that I care about him, too?"

"That is frankly disturbing, Lizzy. If he does not want to hurt you, he should stop doing hurtful things. It's really that simple."

Elizabeth didn't respond.

Jane drew in a breath. "Well, listen, there is no point in talking about it anymore. He has turned your head for some reason. He has toyed with your heart and confused you. It will all fade if you are away from him. We shall hope there is no babe."

"No, don't hope that," said Elizabeth.

"You want to be trapped with him?"

"I..." She shook her head. "Oh, let us simply go to sleep and cease to speak of all this. In truth, I wish that I had never said anything to you."

Jane wrapped her arms around her and hugged her tightly. "We won't speak, then. I shall be quiet, I promise. I only want you safe and happy, you know."

"I do know." Elizabeth hugged back.

* * *

The wedding was three days away and Elizabeth had not yet begun to bleed.

She wished that she could be certain how late she was, but she had not kept strict track of it, unfortunately. She had sat down, looking at a calendar, trying to remember specifically when it had been that she last bled, but it had never seemed truly important before, so she had never paid it much mind.

Now, she could not be sure.

It might be only days late, in which case it might not be late at all, for one thing she knew about her own cycle was that it was often off a few days here and there. This, too, was another reason not to keep strict track, because she couldn't be sure, not down to the day, when it would arrive. Jane's was always like the working of a clock, and Elizabeth rather hated her for it just then. She herself seemed to have inherited her mother's cycle. All things considered, Elizabeth supposed she was glad to have inherited that from her mother in lieu of a great many other things.

She tried to feel sorry about the prospect of being with child and found she could not.

She was frightened, but she wanted the babe.

And the more she thought about it all, the more she began to think that she was selling Mr. Darcy short. Yes, he had raged at her, and he had been horrible to her. But he had never hurt her physically.

And he was different. When he wasn't in pain, he was in better spirits. Even when he was, he had done things like pardoning poor Lady, realizing it wasn't the dog's fault. He had changed, and neither she nor him had given him credit for that.

She wanted the babe. She wanted Mr. Darcy. She wanted it all badly.

"What are you thinking of?" said Lydia.

Elizabeth started. She was in the sitting room, a book open on her lap, but she had not been looking at the pages in quite some time. "I am reading," she said.

" No, you are not, " said Lydia. " Anymore than I am doing embroidery."

Elizabeth looked at Lydia's embroidery, which was frightfully free of stitches.

"So," continued her sister, "what are you thinking of?"

"Nothing," said Elizabeth.

"Are you thinking of your husband?" Lydia smiled brightly. "Is he really as bad as everyone says? He seemed to always be in a bad temper whenever I saw him."

"I was not thinking of him," said Elizabeth.

"I think I should like to marry a man like that," said Lydia.

"What?" said Elizabeth. "A man who is always in a bad temper? Why would you say such a thing?"

"I simply think that everything in a marriage like that must be … heightened. Everything would be very exciting and quite dangerous."

"Lydia, you are not speaking sense."

"La, that is all anyone ever says to me." Lydia shrugged, plunging her needle into the fabric on her lap. "I care not what anyone thinks. I know what I would like, and that is for falling in love to be a great adventure. I want to find a man that no one else can handle and bring him to heel, as if he were a horrid beast."

"Oh, Lydia, please."

"Afterward," said Lydia, "I should like it very much if he were still horrid and frightening to everyone else, but if he were sweet with me."

"Yes," Elizabeth muttered. "Like a guard dog, I suppose."

Lydia tittered. "No, no, a wolf. A tamed wolf."

"A wolf would make for an awful husband."

"I would bend him to my will and he would worship me."

"You are very young, and you have no idea how the world works. Men aren't that way at all."

"Whatever do you mean?"

"They don't worship you. They simply … use you for whatever it is they want you for and then they leave on terribly important business that they won't even explain to you."

"Oh, my," said Lydia, winking. "Is that what happened

to you with your husband?"

"No, never mind me." Elizabeth picked up her book and tried to focus on the words.

"You ought to try harder to bend him to your will," said Lydia. "Have you tried at all?"

"Please stop talking."

"You know, it's funny," said Lydia. "I rather always was certain that I would be the first of the Bennet sisters to get married."

"You are the youngest. How could you get married first?"

"Even so, I was assured of it." Lydia shrugged again. "Ah, well. Since I am not to marry first, I am determined to wait until I find a man who fits my exact specifications. I will settle for nothing less than perfection."

* * *

The morning of the wedding, Elizabeth's bleeding came.

She was shocked to see it at that point. She had been so sure that it wasn't coming that she had been mentally counting the months until she would be showing and would have to be out of society. She had been planning the kind of crib she wanted made for the baby, planning out a set of small baby clothes to dress her tiny child in.

But there was no child.

There was, quite simply, nothing tying her to Fitzwilliam Darcy at all.

She wanted to tell Jane the news, but she had no chance to be alone with her sister that morning. There were servants about, helping her sister get ready, and being called away constantly by their mother, who seemed more worried about the way she would look at the wedding than her own daughter.

Jane was beautiful in her dress. She wore her hair twisted around her head so that it nearly resembled a crown, and Elizabeth had never seen her so radiant.

The wedding was lovely too. She watched Mr. Bingley's

face as Jane walked down the aisle, how he was eager and awed by her sister. He never took his eyes off her throughout the vows. He gazed at her with unabashed adoration.

Elizabeth tried to remember how Mr. Darcy had looked at her during their wedding, but she could not remember his looking at her at all. However, she hadn't spent much time looking at him either.

However, she had seen the same look in Mr. Darcy's eyes, had seen it when they were making love in the east wing, when the lightning illuminated his face.

He loves me, she thought.

Yes, but if he loved her, why had he not said it? When she told him her feelings, he simply argued with her about it.

Before, when there was a possibility of a babe, there was a chance that this decision would be made for her. She would be forced to remain married to him. Now, however, she would have to decide. She did not want the responsibility.

She did not know how to decide.

It was head versus her heart, and she did not know which would win out.

Somehow, at the wedding breakfast, she ended up seated next to Miss Caroline Bingley, and somehow, Miss Bingley was in a talkative mood.

"How does Mr. Darcy?" said Miss Bingley.

"Oh, he is well enough," said Elizabeth.

"I thought he must be ill," said Miss Bingley. "The Mr. Darcy that I knew would never have missed my brother's wedding. He is much changed, however."

"I suppose so," Elizabeth allowed.

"Not that I concern myself with Mr. Darcy," said Miss Bingley. "Indeed, I never think of him anymore. He is quite definitely the furthest thing from my thoughts at practically all times."

Elizabeth only nodded. She had forgotten that Miss

Bingley used to carry a torch for Mr. Darcy.

"At one time, of course, there was much to recommend him, but none of that is true anymore. Why, I remember how he was always so shy and quiet. People thought him arrogant, but it was often that he simply did not feel comfortable in the company of people he did not know very well. I always felt sorry for him and would do my best to try and draw him out when I could. But then, after he was scarred and hurt, nothing could still his tongue. The awful things he said! Of course, I suppose you know. You are married to him. You must hear him say horrible things all the time."

Elizabeth thought of Mr. Darcy's teeth bared, his eyes flashing. *I will have nothing of his in my house.* She inclined her head. "I would not speak ill of my husband when he is not here to defend himself."

"Oh, well would he defend himself?" said Miss Bingley. "The Mr. Darcy I knew was not likely to speak in his own defense. He would have thought that uncouth. He was the very picture of civility, you know. And his sister, the sweet Miss Darcy? Oh, how he loved her. When he would speak of her, something would come over him. You could see how much he cared for her, how he would do anything for her. And then she was lost, and it turned him inside out. Now, he's just a shell of himself."

Elizabeth didn't say anything.

"It's very sad," continued Miss Bingley. "You do have my sympathies, Mrs. Darcy. I think it all must be very difficult for you. That's why I wouldn't trade places with you for all the gold in England."

"Well, I don't believe anyone has asked you to trade places with me."

"Of course not, but it's only that if I imagine your position, I feel as though I have been spared a difficult fate. You may not know this, but at one time, I think it was quite likely that Mr. Darcy might have asked for my hand. I mean, before the accident, when his face was lovely to look on."

" I cannot say that I think the scars have spoiled his looks," Elizabeth muttered.

"Oh, but you don't know what he looked like before," said Miss Bingley. "You may have married him, but you didn't marry the real him. He's nothing but a pale shadow of the man he was. You can't imagine what sort of man he was, back when I..." She shook her head. "Well, anyway, there's no point in dwelling on the past, is there?"

"Indeed, it seems to me that you are the one who seems to continue harping on it."

"Harping?" Miss Bingley drew herself up. "Now, how is that fair? I am merely expressing my sympathy for you. I am extending a bit of Christian charity, and you are throwing it in my face. Perhaps being around Mr. Darcy's bad temper has rubbed off on you."

Elizabeth plastered a smile on her face and changed the subject. "Wasn't it sweet to see the way your brother could not take his eyes off my sister? I think they will be very happy together, don't you?"

Miss Bingley pursed her lips. "Yes, my brother is rather taken with Miss Bennet, I must say."

"With Mrs. Bingley," Elizabeth corrected, smiling wider.

"Well, I hope they suit," said Miss Bingley. "I can't think of anything worse than a marriage between people who don't seem to like each other. Your parents aren't that way, are they?"

Elizabeth glared at her.

It was Miss Bingley's turn to smile, too sweetly.

Elizabeth narrowed her eyes. " Well, out of my own Christian charity, Miss Bingley, I do hope that you find a husband soon. How many Seasons have you been out in society, after all?"

Miss Bingley let out a forced laugh. "Oh, don't worry about me, Mrs. Darcy, though I thank you deeply for your concern."

"Mmm," said Elizabeth. "And I thank you as well."

* * *

Days passed, and Elizabeth found life at her family's home rather trying. She did not know how she had borne living with her mother's shrill voice for all these years. Jane was gone with her new husband, of course, and it left Elizabeth with only her younger sisters and her parents.

Her father was nowhere to be found, as per usual, and her mother turned every little thing into an incident, even the loss of an embroidery needle, for which everyone in the house—the servants and the sisters—spent an entire morning searching every nook and cranny.

Elizabeth retreated into the corner of the sitting room with a book, and she longed for the quiet of Pemberley.

Was it folly if she chose being with Mr. Darcy simply to escape this chaos?

He had promised her that he would give her the means to escape on her own, of course, so she should not allow that to factor into her decision.

She tried to examine whether she missed the man himself or not, and she found that she did.

The problem, she thought, was that it was impossible to reason oneself in or out of love. Love happened, and it wasn't rational or ordered. It was messy and confusing. It descended upon a person, and then that person was at its mercy.

But she supposed that she could accept that. It was only that she rather blamed herself for having fallen in love with Mr. Darcy at all, for she didn't feel he deserved her love. She could not understand why she would love a man such as him. It didn't make sense, and it made her feel out of control.

Yes, that was precisely the sticking point.

Mr. Darcy had forced her to marry him. He had taken away her choice.

Now, it seemed as if she had been robbed of her choice again, by the feelings that she had developed.

She felt as though she were the plaything of fate, like something in one of those awful Greek tragedies.

In those sorts of stories, no matter what a person did, he couldn't escape his fate. The more he tried to get free, the more he was enmeshed in it.

She had a choice. Leave Mr. Darcy behind and start her own story or go back to him.

The choice should free her. Now, she had the opportunity to decide, the whole world spread out in front of her, nothing but possibilities.

But there was no freedom at all in it, because she couldn't chose. The choice plagued her, a demon insect that needled her.

And then, nearly a week after the wedding, she received a letter from Mrs. Peters at Pemberley.

The housekeeper wrote that Mr. Darcy had come home from his business terribly ill, in a raving fever, and that the doctor was not sure if he would recover. Mrs. Peters wrote that Mr. Darcy sometimes called for her in his sleep.

In that moment, suddenly everything was clear.

It wasn't that she needed to choose. That was not what plagued her. What plagued her was that she had already decided, had known it for some time. There had been no question about whether or not she would go back to Mr. Darcy. Of course she would. She loved him, after all.

Perhaps it was unforgivable, and perhaps she was stupid. Other people might not understand her choice, but she had to be true to herself, and this was what she knew in her heart to be right. Perhaps, up until now, she had been too ruled by everyone else's opinions—Mr. Darcy's, Jane's, her father's. But it wasn't their life or their decision. This was hers, and she trusted her own feelings.

She had to go to him now, and nurse him back to health.

She stuffed the letter into her pocket and went upstairs to her room. She began to pack.

CHAPTER NINETEEN

"Lizzy?" came her father's voice from the doorway to the bedchamber.

She looked up, a pale blue evening dress in one hand. "Papa? What are you doing here?" She rarely saw her father prowling about in this part of the house during the day.

"You are leaving, then?" said her father. "I was told you received a letter, and now I find you here, packing your own clothes."

"I did not want to take the servants away from their tasks," said Elizabeth. "I can manage it myself."

"He has summoned you back, then?"

"No, he is ill. It was the housekeeper who wrote, telling me that he is in need of me."

Her father drew in a deep breath. "Listen, Lizzy, I feel wretched. I keep thinking of what happened, and I think that I didn't fight hard enough to convince you not to marry that man. I knew it wouldn't be good for you, and I wanted to stop it, but I'm afraid there is a defect within me somewhere, and I am always taking the easier path. I want to fight, I do, but I crumple under pressure. I should not have crumpled this time."

"Papa, it is all right." She smiled at her father. "He loves me."

"If he loved you, he would have asked you to marry him instead of taking away your choice. There is precious little a woman has in this world, but she is always able to deny a suitor. If he had asked you, what would you have said?"

She shrugged. "I don't know. I may have refused him. But I may not have. You must see that he was a rather better alternative to Collins."

"Yes, but my Lizzy, my wild and headstrong girl, you have never been one to compromise."

"I know," she said. "I am stubborn." She fingered the edge of her dress and then she set it on the bed. "He offered to let me go, you know. He said that he would give me an annulment, and a hefty settlement besides, and that I could be a free and wealthy woman."

"And yet you return to him?"

"Well, he is very ill, Papa. I suppose there is some chance of his not recovering, and then how could that all be arranged, but that is not why I go. The truth is, when I thought of the prospect of his dying, it hurt me so deeply that I knew..." She sighed, her eyes stinging a bit. "I love him. I cannot bear the thought of losing him."

"Truly?" Her father searched her expression.

"Truly."

Her father drew back slowly. "Well, I must admit, that's not what I expected to hear from you. But perhaps I ought to have suspected something when you were willing to wed him at all. I have long known that my Lizzy is not one to do anything she does not wish to do."

Elizabeth laughed a little. "Well, I suppose you are right in that."

"It's only that I don't understand how you've grown up so quickly. A married woman." He shook his head. "I remember when you would run to me and I would catch you up in my arms." He sighed. Then he started out of the room. "All right, then, well I suppose I'll go and sent for a servant to help you pack. You'll need it."

"Thank you, Papa."

He pointed at her. "I still don't like him."

Elizabeth laughed again. "Noted."

"But... perhaps he is a good man who made a mistake."

A great many mistakes, she thought, but she only nodded. "Yes."

* * *

Two days ' journey went slowly under gray skies. Elizabeth was worried that it would snow, because the sky seemed to threaten it, and she knew that a snowstorm might keep her in an inn for days. She worried about what might happen to Mr. Darcy in that time.

But finally, she arrived, and the carriage pulled up to the great house on the hill. Pemberley was as shrouded in mists as ever and the trees seemed even darker and more sinister than they ever had. She disembarked from the carriage to be met by the staff, who had assembled to see her.

" Where is he? " said Elizabeth. " I must go to him at once."

" That ' s just it, Mrs. Darcy, " said Mrs. Peters. " We received your letter only today, and I know not of what you wrote. I have not written to you, mum. Mr. Darcy is not ill. Indeed, he is not here. He is still away on business in the north."

Elizabeth furrowed her brow. "You did not send a letter to me?"

"No," said Mrs. Peters.

"But then, how…?" This was all very strange.

" Shall we get you inside, mum? We have prepared a lovely dinner for you. It will be ready in only a few hours."

Elizabeth let herself be led into the house, but when the footmen brought in her trunk, she stopped them so that she could go through it and find the letter that Mrs. Peters had sent. She handed it to her.

Mrs. Peters looked it over. "What is this?"

"Is that not your signature?" Elizabeth pointed.

" This is not my hand," said Mrs. Peters. "I do not form my letters in this way."

Elizabeth snatched it back. " I suppose I have not ever seen your handwriting." She gazed at the letter. "Who wrote

166

this?"

"Well, I must say that the handwriting looks a bit familiar, but I don't know if I can place it," said Mrs. Peters, tapping her chin. "One of the children's tutors, perhaps? But that doesn't make sense. None of them are here anymore, and haven't been for years."

"You recognize it," murmured Elizabeth, turning the letter over in her hands as if some clue was to be found on the back of it. "But then..." She sighed. "Well, have you heard from Mr. Darcy? He is well?"

"As near as we know, mum," said Mrs. Peters. "He took Mr. Jones with him, and Mr. Jones will keep us apprised if anything were amiss." Mr. Jones was the valet. "Wouldn't you like to go to your room for a bit, then?"

Elizabeth nodded absently, pulling off her traveling gloves. Then she thought she caught sight of movement through one of the doorways to the left. She started in that direction. It was probably one of the servants cleaning. She wasn't sure why she needed to inspect it, but something about all of this was troubling her.

"Mrs. Darcy, where are you going?" said Mrs. Peters, rushing after her.

"Who is in that drawing room?" Elizabeth pointed.

"Why, no one," said Mrs. Peters.

Someone stepped through the doorway. He was tall with golden, curly hair and twinkling blue eyes. He had an insouciant grin on his face, as if he'd just heard a very amusing jest.

"Georgie!" said Mrs. Peters. "You were supposed to stay out of sight. You promised."

"Georgie?" said Elizabeth slowly. Her eyes widened. "Mr. Wickham!"

CHAPTER TWENTY

The blond man laughed. "I see my fame precedes me. But I'm afraid I do not know you."

"This is the mistress of the house, Mrs. Darcy," said Mrs. Peters.

"Yes, of course," said Mr. Wickham, bowing. "So nice to make your acquaintance. You are lovely, may I say?"

Mrs. Peters turned to Elizabeth. "I'm sorry. Georgie dropped by out of nowhere, and with the master away, well…"

Elizabeth gave Mrs. Peters a shrewd look. "Your master did not wish to have this man's dog about, and yet you invite him into the drawing room?"

"Well, the master is always in a temper," said Mrs. Peters. "They were boys together, weren't they? And we all did love Georgie. I'm sure Mr. Darcy's being overly harsh."

Elizabeth eyed Mr. Wickham. "I assure you, he is not. I suppose Mr. Darcy didn't tell you what Mr. Wickham did to Miss Darcy? If he had, you would never have let him across the threshold."

Mr. Wickham winked at Elizabeth. "Fitzie exaggerates. Always has. It's a fault."

"Exaggerates?" said Elizabeth.

Mr. Wickham turned smiling eyes on Mrs. Peters. "Be a dear, would you? Bring us some refreshment? Mrs. Darcy must be famished after her long journey."

"Oh, yes, what am I thinking?" Mrs. Peters smiled. "I'll see to it myself. Do you still like those honeycakes,

168

Georgie?"

"Love them," said Wickham.

Mrs. Peters scurried off.

Elizabeth turned to see if any of the servants were nearby, but the two footmen had taken her trunk up the stairs, and there was no one.

Wickham's hand shot out and he grabbed her arm. He pulled her into the drawing room and he shut the door. He was still smiling. "What was it that Fitzie said to you about me, my dear?"

"Take your hand off me," said Elizabeth. Her heart was rising in her chest, going far too fast. She wasn't sure what she'd expected from George Wickham, but the fact that he was so handsome and smiling made it all worse, somehow.

"Tell me," he said.

"Please," she said. "I'll scream."

He laughed. "Scream, and I shall strike you."

She flinched. She didn't mean to, but she couldn't help it.

Wickham let go of her. "There, now, we're past the point in which I can play it all off, aren't we? It doesn't matter what he said. I doubt I shall convince you that I am not dangerous."

She licked her lips, her hand going back behind her to the doorknob.

He stopped her. "Now, now, Mrs. Darcy. We are in the middle of a conversation. Don't be rude and try to run off. I can't have that. I'll have to stop that."

"You sent me the letter," she said.

"Oh, you're catching onto that, are you?" He clapped a little, politely, as if she had played something very nice on the piano-forte. "Yes, I did arrange this. I did not know about you when I put out the word that I was in the north and he should come and find me. I thought simply to get into the house without Mr. Darcy about and to see what I could arrange on my own. But then I found out he had married, and I had to meet you. I must say, you're too smart to have been trapped in a marriage with our Fitzie."

"Stop calling him that." So, the business to the north, that had been Mr. Darcy looking for Mr. Wickham?

Wickham laughed again. "Oh, my, you actually like him. I always thought he was frightfully dull, and most of the girls we met preferred me. That's one of the reasons he never cared for me. Here I was, better at him at everything, and yet he was the one who'd inherit. Can you believe that? It's ridiculous."

"That's not true," she said.

"Well, it will all be set right soon enough," said Wickham.

"What do you mean?"

"Well, you're here, which is good, because I've already sent him a letter telling him that I have you and the things that we've done together, and—"

"You blackguard!" She shook her head. "Did you actually hurt Georgiana, or did you just pretend?"

"Oh, simply because you and I haven't done these things yet, doesn't mean we won't." He winked at her. "If you're a bit... reluctant, you needn't worry. I actually find that rather exciting."

She shook her head. He couldn't do this. The servants wouldn't obey him. They would obey her. Wouldn't they?

"You might try to convince me you're enjoying yourself, though," said Wickham, eyeing her. "If you please me, Mrs. Darcy, perhaps I'll keep you." He looked her over in such a way that she felt as if his very gaze had somehow violated her.

She wanted to cry. She didn't dare. "I won't."

"We'll get to all that," he said. "For now, you'll only need to invite me to dinner when Mrs. Peters comes back in."

"I would never do such a thing," she said.

"You will, or I will strike you," he said conversationally.

"No," she said, setting her teeth.

He hit her.

She'd never been struck before, and she was unprepared for what it might feel like. He hit her with the flat of his palm, straight across her face, and a crack echoed through the room, and the pain stung and bloomed into her jaw and her teeth and then tears spilled out of her eyes unbidden.

She clutched her hurt face, horrified.

"I can hit you again," he said, studying his fingernails. "But I won't if you invite me to dinner."

"If you hit me in front of Mrs. Peters—"

"I can hit Mrs. Peters too. I can tie her up if I have to. She is certainly not going to stand in my way, but if I do hit her, you'll have the knowledge that it's your stubbornness that has brought that pain upon her."

Elizabeth was shaking all over.

The door opened and Mrs. Peters was there, along with one of the maids, and they had brought tea and honeycakes and bread and butter.

Elizabeth drew herself up. "Mr. Wickham, won't you stay for dinner?"

He smiled like a preening cat. "Why, I would be delighted, Mrs. Darcy. How good of you to ask."

* * *

Elizabeth sat in the drawing room stiffly, holding tea that she wasn't drinking, while Wickham spoke to her about things he and Mr. Darcy had done when they were boys.

"We used to run all over this room," he said, gesturing about casually. "And then, once, we knocked over a vase. It used to sit right here." He pointed. "It shattered into a million pieces and Mrs. Darcy—that's not you, of course, my dear—was quite put out and banned us from coming into the room at all."

Elizabeth let him prattle on until he'd drunk up all his tea. Then she stood up. "You'll want to dress for dinner. I think one of the footman can assist you if you do not have your own valet."

Wickham laughed. " Me? A valet? Well, valets require money, don't they, Mrs. Darcy, and I have been deprived —"

"Yes, well, that is why I shall offer you a servant," she said. "I must get ready as well." She bobbed an almost curtsy to him. "I shall see you soon, Mr. Wickham."

He let her leave the drawing room, and she went to one of the footman and told him to help Wickham dress for dinner, saying that he could use Mr. Darcy's clothes if necessary.

Elizabeth waited until Mr. Wickham and the footman disappeared into one of the guest rooms and then Elizabeth hurried down the servants steps into the kitchen.

Mrs. Peters was at the foot of the steps. "Mrs. Darcy! What are you doing down here?"

"There's not a moment to lose, Mrs. Peters," said Elizabeth. "We must gather up all the servants so that I can speak to you all." She turned. "Miss Jennings, can you go and fetch anyone who is not here?"

"Yes, mum." Miss Jennings hurried up the steps.

"Is this about Georgie?" said Mrs. Peters, looking a bit worried.

Elizabeth didn't answer her. She wasn't sure what to do about Mrs. Peters. Perhaps Mr. Darcy had been right to be angry with her about the dog. Perhaps she'd kept the thing out of some perverse affection for Mr. Wickham. It remained to be seen how deeply she'd hold onto that affection.

Within several moments, the downstairs was full of servants. The footman stood on the steps, peering down, and everyone else gathered around.

Elizabeth called for the cook and the kitchen maids to come out.

"If I come out there, things may burn!" called the cook.

"It's all right," said Elizabeth. "Dinner is truly the least of our worries."

The cook came out, giving Elizabeth a formidable look.

Elizabeth took a deep breath. "I assume that Mr. Darcy

never spoke to you all about Mr. Wickham?"

No one answered for several moments, as if they were afraid to speak.

One of the footmen finally did. "Mr. Darcy has made it plain that we are never to speak about Mr. Wickham."

"Yes," said Elizabeth. "This I know. But certainly, there has been some discussion of what happened. I know that rumors fly within a household and that there are rumors abroad about the two of them. Why, I had it that Mr. Darcy had murdered Mr. Wickham, but we can all see that he is very much alive. Have you heard nothing, then?"

More silence.

" Well, you must have thought that Mr. Darcy had a reason," said Elizabeth. She was trying to ascertain what sort of resistance there was going to be to her proclamation of Mr. Wickham as a rank villain. Many of these people had known him as a boy. They might not be quick to turn against him, and she could see that Wickham had his charms.

" Of course, " said Miss Jennings. " We ' ve had conversations amongst ourselves. We know that Mr. Wickham had been turned away here when he came inquiring for more money. He complained rather loudly to anyone that would hear him that Mr. Darcy had swindled him out of his position in the parsonage."

" That ' s a lie, " said Elizabeth. " Mr. Darcy gave Mr. Wickham the value of that living and Wickham used it all up."

" Truly no one knows what happened, " spoke up Mr. Marshall. "If you do know, mum, please share with us."

"That is what I have called you here for," said Elizabeth. "No matter what love you may bear for Mr. Wickham, I ask you to put it aside for a moment and consider that he has tricked you. When he and I were alone in the drawing room just this afternoon, he struck me and forced me under threat of more violence to invite him to dinner. It was he who wrote me a letter, pretending to be Mrs. Peters, in order to get me back here. He plans to use me against Mr. Darcy, and we cannot let him."

"What?" said Mrs. Peters. "Now, this is preposterous. Why would he do such a thing?"

"I don't know exactly," said Elizabeth, "but I suspect it's got something to do with money. He was so desperate for money that he maneuvered Miss Darcy into eloping with him, after all. And then he ravished her and beat her, and when Mr. Darcy attempted to save her sister, Wickham took Miss Darcy and ran, and then the accident happened."

"No!" said Mrs. Peters. "Georgie would never hurt Georgiana! And she was like a sister to him. He wouldn't..." She put her fingers to her lips. Her hands were shaking. "Oh, dear. Oh, dear."

"Here's what we must do," said Elizabeth. "If you believe me, we must overpower Mr. Wickham when he is not expecting it. All of the footmen must help, I believe, and any other able man. We must restrain him and keep him someplace where he cannot escape until Mr. Darcy arrives and we see what can be done with him." She looked around at all of them. "Will you do as I say? Do you believe me?"

None of the servants said anything.

Elizabeth drew in a shaking breath. "I hesitate to... well, it is not something I would like to reveal, but ... " She swallowed. Her voice trembled. "Mr. Wickham has threatened me as well. Threatened to... to ravish me also, I believe because he knows it would pain Mr. Darcy, and—"

"That's it," called a voice.

Everyone turned to see Mr. Nelson, who was seated in one of the corners. His broken leg was bound in a brace and he had a crutch. He pushed himself up on it. "If none of you will do it, then I shall do it on my own. We won't let anything happen to Mrs. Darcy, will we?"

"No," said Mr. Marshall. "We won't." He turned to look at the footmen. "Come, men, we must restrain this villain at once."

Elizabeth looked at Mrs. Peters, waiting for the woman to object.

But Mrs. Peters' eyes were very wide, and she had both of her hands pressed against her lips. She looked scandalized.

Mr. Marshall nodded at Mr. Nelson. " Don ' t injure yourself further, if you please."

"I wouldn't mind if I had to," said Mr. Nelson, but he sat back down.

Mr. Marshall turned to Elizabeth. "Where shall we put him?"

"Is there an appropriate cellar?"

" No, the root cellar is not securable, " said the cook. "And down here, it is all servants' quarters."

Elizabeth twisted her hands together. "The, um, the east wing, then. We'll put him there."

"Very good, mum," said Mr. Marshall, and he beckoned the other men, who all trooped up the steps.

CHAPTER TWENTY-ONE

Wickham threw out punches, and a few of them collided with the servants, but there were far too many men, and he was rather easily contained.

They tied him and placed him in the east wing.

Once he was contained, he grew piteous. "This is no way to treat a guest, Mrs. Darcy. I see your husband has poisoned you against me, and for no reason. He has always been harsh with me out of jealousy." He turned to the footmen who were still there. "Don't listen to her. She doesn't know what she's saying."

Mr. Marshall shook his head at him. "George, it's no good. I, for one, remember the way your eyes followed little Miss Darcy, and I said to myself then that you were above your station. I have told you time and again that it does no good to reach for what you cannot have."

Wickham sniffed.

"She was just a little girl," said Mr. Marshall. "You ought to be ashamed of yourself."

Wickham fell into a sullen silence for a while, until they all made to leave, and then he began to cry out that he couldn't be left up here in the cold with nothing to eat. "Why, I'd be better treated in a dungeon," he protested.

So, a fire was built and a chamber pot brought and some bread and cheese as well.

A guard was left to make sure he didn't escape.

The servants tried to convince her she should take some sustenance then, but she didn't think she could eat. She was more concerned with making certain that Mr. Darcy was on his way home. She believed that Wickham had sent his dreadful letter, and that should draw Mr. Darcy home soon, but she sent someone after him anyway, to tell him the truth of the matter and to urge him hence, if indeed he needed urging.

She barely slept that night.

The following day, the doctor arrived to check on the progress of Mr. Nelson's leg, and he inquired after her as well.

Elizabeth found herself spilling the entire story to him, asking for his advice on what to do. "What Mr. Wickham did to Miss Darcy is certainly a crime, is it not? If I were to call for the magistrate, they would take him to a prison, and he would receive a harsh sentence."

"One would think," said the doctor sadly.

"What do you mean?" she said.

"Well, I have heard that sometimes a woman can have a man punished for his ravishment of her, but in this case, Miss Darcy had consented to marry him."

"Yes, but that was under false pretenses, and she was so young, she could not have known what she was consenting to."

"Yes, well, a man has a right to his wife, that is what Mr. Wickham's lawyer will say. And furthermore, Miss Darcy is no longer with us to accuse him, so it is not even her word against his, but no word at all."

"Mr. Darcy may yet have the letter in which Wickham admits it all."

"Even so, Mrs. Darcy, I think it would be a rather difficult thing to prove, and it would drag the Darcy name into the muck. No, if you want my advice, I'd call in the law and tell him that he was thieving your horses. They'd string him up for that straightaway."

Elizabeth let out a little noise. "Is a horse worth more than a woman, sir?"

"It's a sad world, my dear," said the doctor.

* * *

It was the middle of the night when Mr. Darcy arrived.

She awoke to a burst of light coming in from the hallway, and she sat up in bed. He was there, looking disheveled. His coat was wet and his hair was plastered against his forehead, and he was limping.

"I told you she is all right, sir," came the voice of Mrs. Peters from the hallway. "Did Mr. Tolson not find you then, sir? Are you come on the word of Mr. Wickham only?"

Elizabeth got out of bed and came across the room to wrap her arms around him.

He was senseless, standing there, unmoving as she embraced him.

Elizabeth looked over his shoulder at Mrs. Peters, who was in her nightgown. "It's all right, Mrs. Peters. You may go. Would you mind lighting a candle for us, however, before you do?"

"Certainly, mum," said Mrs. Peters, who did so.

Elizabeth pulled back to look at Mr. Darcy.

He looked her over. "I've gotten you wet."

"It is raining, sir?"

"It was, I think. I know not. I've been riding straight for two days." He shook his head. "Why are you here? If he did not… capture you, why…?"

"Well, I live here, husband." She put her hand on his cheek.

"There is a babe?"

"No," she said. "There is not."

"You came back?" He gave her a wondering look.

"I did," she said.

"But why did you come back?" He looked at her as if it was incomprehensible.

"Fitzwilliam, I told you that I loved you, did I not?"

He swallowed, looking down at the ground. "You would not lie to me about it, would you?"

"About loving you? Why would I—

"About *him*." His voice was harsh.

She flinched a little at how harsh.

"Did he kidnap you and... and touch you and you are you hiding it from me because you think I couldn't bear to know it?"

"No," she said, shaking her head. "Why would I do such a thing? I know you are strong, sir. Did I not tell you that upon only a short acquaintance?"

He turned toward the door. "I need to see him."

"Now?"

"Yes, now. You know where Wickham is, do you not?" He sagged onto his cane.

"You said you have been riding for days in the rain. Certainly, you should rest. We have the servants guarding him, and he is not going anywhere—"

"Where is he?"

"Please, Fitzwilliam, you are in no condition to—"

"I'm not such a poor excuse for a man that I can't face him. Mrs. Peters says he is tied up. You think I can't look upon a man who is bound hand and foot? I wonder at your declaration of love. You obviously think nothing of me."

"Oh," she said, her nostrils flaring. "That is the second time you have thrown my love for you in my face. Do not do it again. I will not stand for it. You have your own troubles with your low opinion of yourself, sir. I refuse to share them. Hate yourself if you must, but don't try to make me hate you, because I have tried, and I can't."

He gave her an odd look.

She folded her arms over her chest. "If you must go to him, give me a moment to dress. I will come with you."

He shoved the hair on his forehead up and it stuck there because it was wet and stiff with the grime of the road. "You... you are dazzling, Mrs. Darcy. Has anyone ever told you this before?"

She laughed a little.

"Why did you come back to me?" He shook his head at her, seemingly dazed.

"Give me a moment, sir. I will put something on and we will go to the east wing."

He straightened, and his voice was a steadily rising threat. "You put him in the east wing?"

" Well, " she said, going to her wardrobe, " there was nowhere else."

"But that is... he is *defiling* —"

"I know," she said. "I did not know what else to do with him."

Darcy sighed, his jaw twitching. " He won't say there. There must be somewhere else to put him."

She pulled a dress over her head. It had only a few buttons in the front and she did them up. Tying her hair into a careless knot at the nape of her neck, she presented herself. "All right, let's go, then."

"All right," he said.

As they walked, she told him of her conversation with the doctor, and how he had advised that they turn him over to the authorities for stealing their horses.

"But he didn't steal any horses," Darcy muttered darkly.

"What he's done is far worse," she said, "but it may be harder to have him condemned for such things, so I think it is the best way."

"I'm not having him condemned to death for a lie," said Darcy.

" Sir, I am not one to wish suffering on anyone, even a man like Wickham, but..." She stopped then, twisting her hands together.

Darcy kept going several paces after her before stopping. He was leaning heavily on his cane and limping, but he was moving just the same. He turned to her. "What?"

" Do you remember when we spoke of Iago and Don John in Shakespeare, and I said such men were fictional, that no one hurt people just because they delighted in causing

180

pain?"

"I do," said Darcy.

" Well, whatever Mr. Wickham is, he is … " She swallowed. "He made threats to me, Fitzwilliam, and I could see it all over him. He *does* enjoy inflicting pain. He is some kind of… storybook monster."

" No, Elizabeth, he's a man," said Darcy. " But you're right, he's a different sort of man. I don't know if he could inhabit the pages of a Shakespeare play, but there is something within him that is … wrong. He can be so charming, you know, but it's all a mask."

"Yes," she said. "And underneath, he's horrid."

"Yes," said Darcy.

"Did you know before? Before he took your sister?"

"I…" He grimaced. "I suppose I did not know the depths of his depravity."

"You see, then, Fitzwilliam, you can't blame yourself for not understanding him, for thinking him like other men. It is him you must blame and not yourself."

Darcy sighed heavily and started to walk again.

"Fitzwilliam, wait," she called.

But he kept going.

They did not speak again until they reached the room where Wickham was being kept.

Darcy spoke to the guard at the door, telling the man he could go.

"No," whispered Elizabeth, "what are you doing? Have him stay."

Darcy ignored her and entered the room.

Wickham was lying on the floor, asleep.

Darcy went to him and kicked him. " Wake up, Wickham."

Wickham scrambled up into a crouch, holding his bound hands in front of him. "Fitzie! It's you. You're here."

" I am. " Darcy looked down at him, and in the scant candlelight, with his scars, he was frightful to behold.

181

"I'm glad," said Wickham. "It seems to me that we have a disagreement of sorts, and we should settle it like gentlemen."

"Settle it?" echoed Darcy.

" Yes, " said Wickham. " I challenge you, Fitzwilliam Darcy, to a duel."

CHAPTER TWENTY-TWO

Darcy took a step back, and he had to catch himself on his cane. He wavered, nearly losing his balance.

Wickham laughed. "It's only honorable to accept, Fitzie. If you don't, well, then, what will be said of you? That you're a coward?"

"I suppose you'd want a loan from me of whatever weapon I choose? And I suppose you haven't got anyone to be your second or third either," said Darcy.

"Well, naturally, I'd be dependent on your hospitality."

"Very well," said Darcy. "Swords."

"What?" said Elizabeth. "Are you insane? He is your prisoner, you cannot agree to duel him."

Wickham held up his hands. "Untie me. I need time to prepare. Shall we fight at dawn?"

"Fitzwilliam!" said Elizabeth. "*He* must die. Not you. There must be no chance that anything would happen to you, and we spoke before of duels, about how they were not about justice, but sheer chance. Please."

Darcy did not take his eyes from Wickham. "Elizabeth, you said that you were not with child, so I don't see what you're so concerned about. You mustn't think that you would not be well taken care of. You will be my widow, after all. You think I would not provide for you in the event of my death?"

"You're *not* dying," said Elizabeth. "I don't want you dead. Don't you understand?"

Darcy shook his head. He leaned on his cane. "I can't lie.

I can't have him hung as a horse thief. That's not how this ends."

Wickham looked back and forth between them. "Hang me? Don't be ridiculous, Darcy. You're the one who's wronged me. I'm still grieving over the loss of my wife, and—"

"Have a care," Darcy interrupted him in a quiet voice. "I might change my mind."

"You've already accepted the duel," said Wickham. "It would be dishonorable to back out now. And this is about honor, isn't it, Darcy?"

Darcy chuckled softly, looking Wickham over.

"Come now," said Wickham. "Let me free."

Darcy moved his cane, and then he dragged his feet toward Wickham.

"I can't let you do this," said Elizabeth, and she started forward as well.

"I hardly think you'd be pleased," said Darcy to Wickham. "Whenever we fenced, I always bested you, didn't I? You didn't really think I'd choose pistols?"

Elizabeth approached.

Darcy turned to her, sticking out his cane. "Stay out of this."

She halted, biting down on her bottom lip.

Wickham held his hands up to Darcy.

Darcy fumbled in his jacket and came out with a small dagger. He unsheathed it and cut Wickham free.

Wickham got to his feet, kicking off the remains of the ropes. He sprang across the room and seized Elizabeth.

Elizabeth struggled, but Wickham's grasp was too tight.

Wickham laughed, delighted. "I can't believe you fell for that, Fitzie. Really, you *are* an idiot."

CHAPTER TWENTY-THREE

Elizabeth struggled. She drove her elbow into Wickham. Wickham let out a noise, air going from his lungs.

Elizabeth tried to get away.

But Wickham tightened his arm around her, pulling her back against his body. He moved, one of his arms going about her throat.

She gasped, coughing.

Darcy put his cane down on the floor, and the sound echoed through the room.

Wickham laughed again, but it was thinner now. "I'll crush the life out of her. Don't move."

"I thought you said this was about honor, Wickham," said Darcy.

"Well, it's about yours. I don't have any. Honor is a dreadful inconvenience, you know."

"Indeed." Darcy shook his head. "Let her go."

"You know I can't. She's my shield. No, listen, here's what we'll do. She and I are going to go downstairs, out of this wing, and you'll provide us with a horse—no, that's a bad idea. I won't be a horse thief. A carriage."

"Us?" said Darcy. "You think to take my wife along with you?"

"For leverage, of course," said Wickham. "And perhaps a bit of fun as well. After I've had her, it'll be like the girl in Cambridge, the one I stole from you?"

Darcy bared his teeth.

"We can talk over how wet her cunny was, just as we did

then, and decide to be friends and never let a bit of breasts and hips come between us again," said Wickham.

Elizabeth struggled once more.

Darcy cleared his throat. "I'd rather you didn't speak such vulgarity in front of my wife."

"Well, let me tell you, the vulgar things I'm going to subject her to—" But Wickham stopped speaking.

Because Darcy had taken a pistol out from the folds of his coat.

"Darcy, what are you about?" said Wickham.

"Step away from her," said Darcy, holding the pistol aloft, pointing it directly at Wickham's head.

"You… you wouldn't shoot me," said Wickham, who was all agog over this development.

"I should have brought a loaded gun when I came for Georgiana," said Darcy. "You think I'd make the same mistake twice?"

"Fine," said Wickham, wounded. He let go of Elizabeth and stepped backward, arms up. "There we go, Darcy, it's all right. You're really getting rather worked up, aren't you? How long has it been since you've slept? You look a bit worse for wear." Wickham laughed again, nervous. When Darcy didn't reply, he kept talking. "Well, there it is. I'm no longer touching her. Lower the gun, for God's sake, man. Lower it now."

Darcy pulled the trigger.

CHAPTER TWENTY-FOUR

Elizabeth screamed. She didn't mean to. She wasn't upset at the development, even though Wickham's throat had exploded in red gore, even though he was thrown backward and he twitched twice before he was still.

She was relieved, and she wanted to start crying.

Darcy let his hand holding the pistol drop to his side. Laboriously, leaning heavily on his cane with the other hand, he made his way across the room to Wickham. He nudged the man's body with his foot.

"He's dead," said Elizabeth softly.

Darcy looked up at her.

"Thank you," she whispered.

Darcy let out a breath and a strange noise, reminiscent of a sob. Then he hobbled out of the room.

Elizabeth looked around, at the fire, the chamberpot, the ceiling, everywhere except at the body. And then she followed him.

Darcy walked directly into the wall. He rested his forehead against it, and then his cheek, and then he turned around, his head still touching the wall. With his back to the wall, he slid down to the floor.

His cane dropped with a clatter.

He set the pistol carefully in front of him.

It was quiet.

Elizabeth stood in the doorway to the room where Wickham was.

Movement, at the end of the hallway, servants coming

into the wing. She stepped forward, shaking her head. "Back, go back!" she called at them. "Not yet."

They halted, looking from her to Mr. Darcy.

Darcy waved them off.

Hesitantly, they retreated.

Elizabeth watched them go, and then she sat down in front of Mr. Darcy. She took his hands in hers.

The unscarred side of his mouth quirked up a bit. "I'm sorry you had to see that."

"I'm all right."

"I shouldn't have let you come with me," he said. "I don't know why I did."

She thought of his sending off the guard at the door. "You were planning on killing him all along."

He sighed heavily. "I think perhaps I was."

She squeezed his fingers. " He deserved it. He had nothing but evil to bring to the world."

"I'm sorry that he hurt you."

"I'm all right."

"I'm sorry he said those things in front of you."

"Mr. Darcy, I am fine. I am whole and well."

" You know, I was not in the habit of having horrible discussions with him about women's, er … That thing he said, I was not that sort of man. I was never that sort of man."

"Mr. Darcy," she laughed. "There are great many things that I seem to be able to forgive you. Something that happened when you were barely more than a boy, before you even knew me… I shall never think on it again, and I have never believed a word out of his mouth."

"I don't deserve you."

"No, I don't think you do."

" I love you, though," he said. He winced faintly. "I've never told you that, have I?"

She looked away, suddenly shy.

"I've loved you a long time," he said. "I'm not sure when

it started, but for a great many days and nights, since before your sister fell sick at Netherfield, I have thought of you first when I awoke and last before I went to sleep. And if I have not treated you the way a man should treat a woman he loves, then I must say ... well, I cannot excuse myself, for there aren't excuses. But you are here. You came back. So, I think you might be willing to give me a chance to try to do better?"

"That is exactly why I'm here," she said, smiling.

"I shall," he said, giving her a very serious look. "I swear to you that I shall be a better man from now on."

She squeezed his fingers again.

* * *

Without any real discussion of the matter, the servants hauled Mr. Wickham's body out of the house, and Mr. Nelson loudly proclaimed that he'd been stealing the horses and had been shot in the attempt. "No one will say any different, upon my word," he assured Mr. Darcy.

Mr. Darcy said they could bury Mr. Wickham in the morning. It was too late for any of that now.

Then he and Elizabeth went to his bedchamber, where he washed himself as best he could in a basin, and then, exhausted, he fell into bed, and Elizabeth stayed with him. They didn't discuss that either. She wasn't about to leave his side, and he didn't ask her to.

When she woke in the morning, it was like the first night in the inn, their limbs entangled, his firm warmth wrapped around her. She breathed in the scent of him. She never wanted to let him go.

She studied him in his sleep. He seemed lighter somehow, and she didn't know how. But some burden he'd been carrying had been jettisoned along with that bullet. It wouldn't bring back his sister, and it wasn't justice, not truly, because nothing could make it all right.

But she couldn't be sorry that Mr. Wickham was dead.

She kissed Mr. Darcy's scar, the place where it started,

right at his eyebrow.

His eyes fluttered open.

"Sorry I woke you," she murmured.

"You're here with me," he said, smiling at her.

She smiled back.

He pulled her down and kissed her lips. She clung to him.

"How could I possibly be so lucky as to have you here?" he whispered.

"You know," she said, "you are not really as awful as all that."

He chuckled. "No?"

"No, your wickedness is somewhat exaggerated, I must say. I would not be a wardrobe of dresses or a table set with plates when you are angry, truly, but beyond that, you are all bluster."

Now, he was really laughing.

"I am not frightened of you at all," she said.

"That, my sweet one, is because you have tamed me." He kissed her nose.

She shut her eyes, happy in this moment, and she knew this was where she belonged. She could not be anywhere but by his side. "If I have tamed you, then I command you."

"Yes, absolutely. I am your willing slave. What do you require, Elizabeth?"

It was her turn to laugh. "I shall probably require a great many things. After we break our fast, I shall begin a list. An exhaustive list."

"Mmm," he said. "Planning on keeping me busy, then?"

"Yes," she said. "I think so."

He let out something very like a growl. "I would very much like to be kept busy right now."

"But?" she said. "I sense there is a 'but' coming."

"Well, we do have to deal with the body," he said, and grimness settled over him.

"You're right, of course," she said. It was odd, she would

have thought it monstrous to be thus the morning after a killing a man, but because of the oppressiveness that Wickham had wrought in his wake, it was hard not to feel as if a weight had been lifted now that he was gone.

Wickham had no family. His father, the steward, had passed some years ago, and his mother had died long ago in childbirth. He had no brothers or sisters. So, there was no one to claim him. He was buried quietly and they moved on.

Later that evening, they sat in front of the fire in the main hall, and the dogs lay between them.

Mr. Darcy was absently stroking Lady's head. "Georgiana found them."

Elizabeth, who had been staring into the fire for some time, mesmerized by the patterns of the flames, looked up. "Found who?"

"They were out on the edge of the woods there." Darcy gestured, taking his hand off of Lady. He scratched at the scar on his face.

"Does it itch you?" she said, leaning forward, concerned.

"I prefer it itching to hurting," he said, giving her a half smile.

"What are you talking about?" she said. "What did your sister find?"

"Oh, the puppies," he said. "She was small then. Only about eight years old. Our parents were both gone by then. I think it was only a month after my mother's funeral."

Elizabeth looked at him, her heart going out to him. So much suffering in his life, so much pain. "The puppies," she murmured. Then she looked at Lady. "Oh, the dogs!" She understood now. "They were puppies then."

His smile widened. "That is generally the nature of dogs, madam."

"Oh, leave off." She narrowed her eyes good-naturedly. "I know what you are speaking of now."

"They were small then," he said, returning to scratch under Lady's chin. "There were three of them, and they were squirming and mewling and half-dead. Their eyes weren't open yet. They were just tiny things. Georgiana was enchanted. She insisted we bring them into the house and find some way to feed them and care for them, and I was worried that one or more of them would die and break her heart all over again. She took the loss of our mother very hard. She was so young, and girls need their mothers." He shook his head.

Elizabeth wanted to touch him, but they were sitting far apart, three large dogs between them.

"They all survived, though, all three of them," said Mr. Darcy. "I remember her deciding which dog belonged to whom." He pointed. "That one over there, Rex, is meant to be mine. But he's never cared for me, I must say. He always loved everyone except me." He laughed.

"Did you name him?"

"Name him? Oh, no." Darcy shook his head. "Just because he was my dog, you mustn't assume that meant Georgiana was willing to relinquish any part of it to me. No, she named them all."

"So, then, Lily was hers." Elizabeth got out of her chair and knelt next to the dog, who was lying on her side, looking into the fire. She rubbed the dog's fur, and Lily closed her eyes in perfect satisfaction.

"Yes." His voice had a catch in it.

Elizabeth looked up at him. "Oh, Fitzwilliam, I…"

"I remember I asked her who Lady would belong to since there were only two of us," said Darcy. "She thought about it, and then she said, seeming very proud of herself, 'Why, she must be Georgie's!'"

Elizabeth got up from petting the dog and went to him. She settled her hand on his shoulder.

"She was good to Wickham. She treated him better than he deserved," said Darcy. "And then, the way he repaid her for that goodness—" His voice broke.

She reached for him.

He clutched at her skirts, and buried his face against her stomach.

He cried.

She held him.

* * *

They went to his bed again not too long later, and they made love for the second time, and this time, Elizabeth thought it really was about comfort. Not just his, either. It was soft and warm and good.

After, cocooned in his arms, she felt safe. He dropped kisses on top of her head, whispering how much he loved her.

She ran her fingers over the scars on his chest.

"So, what do we do now?" he murmured.

" Now, we endeavor to be the least interesting and happiest people in all of Derbyshire," she said.

He chuckled. "All right. I suppose I can attempt that."

" And perhaps we change the draperies in the drawing room on the second floor."

" Oh, really? Now, we discuss decorations? We are that uninteresting?"

" Indeed," she informed him. "We are the dullest of the dull."

He laughed, tangling his fingers in her hair. " Nothing about you is dull. You are brilliant, like a bright and wonderful star."

"Oh, stop it, Mr. Darcy, you will turn my head."

" Well, Mrs. Darcy, you must be attractive enough for both of us, you know. Of the pair of us, you are the only one handsome."

" That is not true. I will never get my fill of looking at you." She smiled up at him.

He kissed her.

She felt lost in the wondrousness of it, their bare skin pressed close under the covers in his bed, being so close to him.

He pulled back, and his voice was dark and rich. "What about the east wing? Ought we discuss decorating that?"

"We don't have to yet," she said. "If you're not ready —"

"I am," he said. "I have other memories of that place now, and it does not hold the same place in my mind."

"Oh, yes," she said quietly, thinking of the fact that it was the place Wickham had been shot.

"I was thinking, darling, of us together in the storm," he murmured.

"Oh," she said in a different voice. "Yes."

"But now that you mention it, I am not sure it is the proper place for a nursery. We'll turn it all into guest rooms and put the new nursery in the west wing."

"You're eager for there to be a nursery, are you?"

"Not if you're not," he said.

"I didn't say I wasn't." She had wanted his babe to be growing in her before, after all.

He touched her cheek. "Well, if that is to happen, I should probably see the doctor sooner rather than later to reset the bone in my leg. Because it takes a frightfully long time to heal, you know."

She lifted up a bit to look down at him. "You're going to do that?"

"Well, if I want to be running after our children, I shall need to get rid of that cane, shan't I?"

"Yes," she whispered. "You will."

CHAPTER TWENTY-FIVE

Elizabeth and Jane had been lax about their letter writing. Elizabeth was willing to forgive all that. Her sister was newly married, after all. But she set about writing letters on her own, one a day, and in them, she told Jane of everything that had happened.

She did not deviate from the story of Wickham being shot stealing horses. It would not do for that letter to fall into the wrong hands, after all. It hardly mattered when and where Mr. Darcy had shot Mr. Wickham, however. It didn't change much of the tale. She told Jane that she was happy, that Mr. Darcy had changed, that she couldn't imagine a better life for herself.

Jane wrote back, cautious about Mr. Darcy but glad her sister was happy. She told Elizabeth of her own life with Mr. Bingley, about hosting dinner parties at Netherfield and how much she was enjoying being the lady of the house.

They wrote often to the other that they needed to see each other soon, so eventually Elizabeth invited them both to Pemberley.

It was springtime and there was no longer the threat of snow making the roads impassable.

Jane and Mr. Bingley arrived one afternoon, their carriage coming under the row of trees that made up the drive to Pemberley. Now that it was spring, the trees were alight in pink buds, and they were beautiful, not the least bit ominous.

Elizabeth received them outside, embracing her sister the

minute she stepped from the carriage.

"But where is Mr. Darcy?" said Jane.

"Oh, he is sitting just inside," said Elizabeth. "He must stay off his leg while it is healing or it won't heal properly, and all this will have been for naught."

"What's this?" said Mr. Bingley.

"Didn't I tell you, Charles?" said Jane, looking up at him. "I thought for sure that I did. A doctor says that Mr. Darcy's leg was set crookedly at first and that he could break it and reset it so that Mr. Darcy would no longer need a cane."

"Oh?" said Mr. Bingley. "Well, capital. That's very good indeed."

They entered the house and Darcy waved to them from his chair. "Bingley, old chap, it's been too long."

Mr. Bingley crossed the room to shake his hand. "I don't think I've heard you sound that pleased about anything in quite some time."

Darcy laughed. "Welcome, both of you. We must go to the second floor drawing room, where my lovely wife has changed the draperies."

"No, there's no reason to go to the trouble of carrying you all the way up there," said Elizabeth. Mr. Darcy could not put pressure on his leg, so in order to get to the second floor, servants had to carry him. "Besides, it's been quite a journey. Perhaps our guests would like to settle into your rooms first."

"Trust me," said Mr. Darcy, "you'll want to see these draperies. They are astounding."

Elizabeth shook her head at him, smiling. "You are incorrigible, Mr. Darcy." She turned to Jane. "Draperies are hardly the most important thing here, are they? Having you here is. Oh, I have missed you."

"And I have missed you, too," said Jane.

* * *

After dinner, Jane sat near the draperies in the second-floor drawing room, looking them over approvingly. "These

196

are lovely."

"Mr. Darcy likes to tease me about them," said Elizabeth. "He couldn't care less about draperies, of course. Men never care about draperies."

"Oh, Mr. Bingley does," said Jane. Then she considered this. "Well, he listens when I speak about them, anyway."

Elizabeth laughed. " I get the impression your husband would listen to you talk about anything at all and with rapt attention. I remember the way he looked at you during your wedding, and he still looks at you that exact same way, as if the sun rises and sets in your eyes."

" He is most attentive, " said Jane, blushing a bit and looking away. But then she looked up. " And your husband... he is different."

Elizabeth nodded. "Yes, he is. But in some ways, he is exactly the same. This is who he always was, underneath it all. He was oppressed by the pain and the sadness of his history. He had a lot of things to work through."

"But you loved him through it all."

Elizabeth shrugged. "I fell in love with him by accident. I certainly didn't mean to. And there were a number of times throughout when I felt it was quite the cross to bear. I would have been happy *not* to be in love with him."

"But no more? Now, you are happy."

"I am very happy."

" Then I am happy for you, " said Jane. " And I feel as though I can finally see the good in Mr. Darcy."

" It can be hard to see at first, I grant you that, " said Elizabeth. " But he *is* good. He is ... quite everything I ever wanted."

* * *

Bingley downed the rest of his brandy in one gulp. "You never told me all this."

" I couldn't, " said Darcy, who had barely touched his drink. The men sat in his study, opposite each other in tall leather chairs. "I simply couldn't say any of it aloud. To do

197

so was to experience it again, to be that failure as a man all over again."

" Ah, of course you saw it that way, " said Bingley. " I wish I had known. I might have been a bit more sensitive with some of the things that I said."

" No, you were rather more patient with me than I deserved, I think," said Darcy. "I was wretched when I came to visit you."

"So, you killed him, and then you restored your faith in yourself, you felt you were a man again."

"No." Darcy shook his head. "I thought that was what I needed, but I was wrong about that. No, that was giving him too much power over me. He had already taken so much from me, and I was letting him have my will and good nature as well. I was letting him utterly destroy me. When I got that letter from him about Elizabeth—"

"That must have been devastating. Lord, you *thought* he had actually done it."

"Well, you know, it was devastating, but it wasn't about me," said Darcy. "That was the hell of it, Charles, this horrid thing happened to my sister, but she was gone, so I couldn't do anything for her. My pain mattered. But Elizabeth was alive, and *she* was all that mattered. *I* didn't matter and how I felt about it didn't matter, and that was when I realized what an idiot I was being. None of it *meant* anything, you understand? He was a... beast. He was a rabid dog, and he'd gotten loose, and he needed to be put down, nothing else. Doing that, it didn't prove anything, and it didn't change anything. It was simply a thing that needed doing."

Bingley nodded slowly.

" Am I making sense of it or am I simply talking in circles?" Darcy took a sip of his brandy.

" No, you're making sense, " said Bingley. " I think I understand. It's only that it's all so awful. The things he did, it makes my skin crawl."

"Indeed." Darcy nodded. "Well, let's cease to speak of

him, then. Shall we find those wives of ours, see the draperies I have so often recommended?"

Bingley laughed. "I must admit, I am becoming overly curious about these draperies. I hope they will not disappoint me."

"Perish the thought," said Darcy. "And if they do, I feel impelled to tell you that I shall disavow friendship with you if you express such an opinion in front of my wife."

"I see, then. You wish me to lie."

"Through your teeth." Darcy lifted his glass of brandy. "But you won't need to, I assure you. They are very fine draperies. That is, I think they are. I own that I have paid little attention to draperies before now, but such are the mysteries and joys of marriage. Cheers."

Bingley laughed. "Indeed, you are right. I would drink to that, but I haven't anything left in my glass."

"And I would fill it for you, but I am unable to stand, considering my leg. " Darcy gestured to it helplessly, shrugged, and tipped the glass into his mouth.

"You may be a beast yet," said Bingley, shaking his head at him.

Darcy grimaced as the strong drink went down. "Depend upon it."

CHAPTER TWENTY-SIX

six months later…

Elizabeth squirmed against her husband in bed as morning light streamed around the draperies.

He tightened one thick arm around her, pinning her against him, making some kind of noise deep in his throat.

The sound was so male, and he was so close, that it went through her, thrilling her in all the right ways. "Let go, sir," she breathed, even so. "I have a great many things that I have to attend to this morning, and we have already slept later than we intended."

"No," he muttered, his mouth against her neck.

She shuddered against the way his breath there made shivers run up her spine. "Stop it. You are making it more difficult than it should be to get out of bed."

"I want you to stay," he said. "You said we couldn't share a bed while we had guests."

She always slept here. After the business with Wickham, she thought they both needed the closeness of the other, and then it had simply become habit. She liked being close to him at night. Furthermore, it was warmer than sleeping alone. "Well, I hardly think it would be proper."

"They don't need to know," he said, sounding petulant. "It's going to be a trying time all around, what with both my aunt and your mother under the same roof."

"True enough," said Elizabeth. "But at least we will not also have Lydia's shrill voice to contend with." Lydia's wedding had been three months before. She had married a man named Cumberville, who was an officer in the regiment. He did not seem to be a wolf, nor did he seem to be bent entirely to Lydia's will either, but Lydia seemed pleased with the situation all the same. At any rate, she was too caught up in her new husband to visit.

"I shall keep you close to me while I can. Why, I shall barely have the chance to touch you while they are here. It will be a very long fortnight, I fear."

"Perhaps it won't be so bad," said Elizabeth. "I'm sure my mother will wish to have Lady Catherine's good opinion."

"Yes, which she will attempt to secure by bragging," said Mr. Darcy.

She chuckled, turning in his arms. "Already, you know my mother so well?"

"I'm sorry," he said, brushing her hair away from her face. "I haven't offended, have I? You know that I love your mother dearly."

She snorted. "Oh, yes?"

"For your sake, my darling, my love, the light of my life."

She kissed his chin, which was a little prickly in the morning. He needed a shave, but she liked seeing him like this. She ran her fingers over his stubble. "You are a wonder, my love."

"And you, of course, will endeavor to love my aunt," he said. "But you will fail, because she is unlovable. Also, she has never gotten over the fact that I had the indecency to become horribly scarred, thereby rendering me unfit to marry her daughter."

"What? You were betrothed? But you never told me."

"I was not betrothed. My mother nodded once when my aunt was prattling over the cradles of myself and Anne, and my aunt decided this was as good as a contract. But then, after the accident, she ceased to speak of it."

"Well, your cousin is likely happy not to be married to

one such as you. Indeed, hasn't she made a very nice match?"

"She has. I'm sure she wakes up every morning and thanks her lucky stars not to be bound to me. In truth, I may have said some very insulting things to her in that period after the accident and before I met you."

"You said insulting things to everyone. Even *after* you met me."

"Well, you were dreadfully slow about reforming me."

"I see." She nodded. "It's my fault. Of course, you would rewrite history to throw off the mantle of blame."

"I'm crippled," he said. "I can't carry any mantles."

She snorted again. He hardly limped anymore.

He groaned, burying his face against her skin. "Do we *have* to get out of bed? Can't we stay here all day? I can think of a great many ways to occupy ourselves."

"They will all be arriving after luncheon, don't be daft."

"No way to put them off?"

"You know very well that I will be unable to accept visitors within a few short months."

"Yes," he whispered, and his mouth moved down her body to plant a kiss on her stomach, which was still mostly flat, with just a tiny hint of the babe that was growing inside her. "Good morning, little one."

She stroked the back of his head.

He looked up at her. "Have I expressed my love for you lately?"

"Not this morning, no," she said.

"I love you," he said, his voice a little rough. "I love you most ardently." He kissed her belly again. "Both of you."

"And I love you, too," she said. "Now let me out of this bed, or I shall be very cross."

"Well, we can't have that," he said. "After all, you are the one with the temper in the household."

"Yes," she said. "A *fearsome* temper."

"I would not stand in your way for all the world."

Made in the USA
Monee, IL
16 July 2020